FUTURE HUMANS

FUTURE HUMANS

GEORGE DEPUY
WITH TIM RAYBORN

PALMETTO
PUBLISHING

Charleston, SC
www.PalmettoPublishing.com

Future Humans
Copyright © 2022 by George DePuy

All rights reserved

No portion of this book may be reproduced, stored in a retrieval system, or transmitted in any form by any means–electronic, mechanical, photocopy, recording, or other–except for brief quotations in printed reviews, without prior permission of the author.

Hardcover ISBN: 978-1-68515-895-8
Paperback ISBN: 978-1-68515-896-5
ebook ISBN: 979-8-88590-120-8

DEDICATION

THE AUTHOR WOULD LIKE TO thank all family members, friends, and collaborators who have supported him on this project. Special thanks go to the creative team of Kathleen, Cam, and Josh for encouraging him to persist. And finally, to Tim Rayborn for bringing the story to life.

TABLE OF CONTENTS

Prologue ·ix
Chapter 1 · 1
Chapter 2 · 17
Chapter 3 · 35
Chapter 4 · 53
Chapter 5 · 71
Chapter 6 · 90
Chapter 7 · 107
Chapter 8 · 124
Chapter 9 · 144
About the Author · 161

PROLOGUE

THIS BOOK HAS BEEN IN process for 45 years. It began with a dream about the future and how people would be living. For more than 30 years I kept a dream journal as a reflective exercise to record insights and think ahead about my personal future and more broadly to that of humanity. As an engineer and academic, I have been well educated in systematic problem solving and found that dream journaling balanced the analytic mind with the art of the possible. I studied futurists who described potential scenarios for humanity. This led to a curiosity about subjects such as climate change, Unidentified Flying Objects, ancient cities and civilizations, symbolic/sacred monuments, and conjecture about time travel. The synthesis of science and creative artistry provided fertile ground to cultivate ideas that grew into this book with its insights for how we humans will face the future with hope and courage. For my grandchildren and theirs, Future Humans was born.

CHAPTER 1

IT HAPPENED AGAIN.

Jace opened his eyes with a start, tumbling out of sleep in an instant. He drew in a sharp breath and tried to make sense of his surroundings. All dark, all quiet, save for the glow of the moon filtering in through the bedroom window. Beside him, Sara slept soundly, at peace. He could see the gentle rising and falling of her breathing.

While she was calm, he was anything but. His heart was racing and he could feel sweat on his head and chest. The dreams had disturbed his slumber once more, dreams that intrigued, beckoned, enticed. He could never quite guess their meaning or their content. In the moment that he returned to the waking world, it was all so clear, but like sand slipping through his fingers, his memories of them faded before he could hold onto them, blown away in the winds of consciousness.

He sighed, and took a few deep breaths to try to calm himself down. He looked at the clock.

3:33, again, he thought, almost with amusement. It was always 3:33 in the morning when he woke up.

He rubbed his hands over his face with some vigor, to try to assure himself that he was really awake, and not simply in another phase of the dream. Confident that he had rejoined the everyday world, he got up and crept to the window, mindful of not disturbing Sara. It was an act he was getting good at, since the dreams came almost nightly now.

But why?

He peered out the window and into the dim light of a pre-dawn summer morning. Beyond the houses across the street was the forest, Fairburn Woods. The moon hung low in the sky like a beacon, showing the way while not quite lighting up the tops of the trees. And in the heart of the woods, there was total darkness. They called to him, these trees. No, something in them did. Something ancient, almost primal, something that seemed connected to the Earth itself. It spoke to him, yearned for him.

This is ridiculous! He shook his head in confusion again. *Every night, what does it mean? Damn it!*

He resisted the urge to pound his hand against the wall, but only just. He looked back to Sara, who slept on, unaware of his turmoil, his confusion.

And that's the way it needs to stay.

Letting out another quiet sigh, he turned to creep into bed and try to force himself back to sleep, but something tugged at him, kept him from taking that easy option. He looked over at their bedroom door, slightly ajar, since it made a creaking noise when shut fully. Over the past few nights, he'd thought of shutting it and locking it from inside, though he didn't know why. It was something to do with the dreams.

The dreams. Visions and flashes of brief moments. Sensations of someone else, some*thing* else, being in the room with him. Maybe several of them. Standing by his bed, observing, watching, like silent sentinels.

How did they get in here? He would ask himself in a half-woken state. *Who? Where?* As always, once alert, the room was empty, quiet. Just as it was now. He thought of Grace and Tom, sleeping in their rooms down the hall. What if something was here? What if something was watching him? Watching them all? Were they in danger? What did it mean?

He swallowed hard and made for the door, not even sure why.

The woods. What's out there?

Sliding into the hall, he was halfway down the stairs before he even thought about what he was doing. He was at the front door, slipping on shoes and a jacket before the absurdity of the whole thing finally caught up with him.

"You're going for a walk, in the damned woods, at 3:30 in the morning," he whispered, realizing how ridiculous it all was as he voiced it aloud. He started to take off his jacket and even slipped out of one shoe, when an urgency, a longing unlike anything he'd ever felt, washed over him.

"No, I *have* to go out there. I have to! Whatever this is, it can't keep going on like this."

Grabbing his keys, he slipped out the front door, shutting and locking it as quietly as possible, and stepped out into the summer night. He took in his surroundings. The air was cool, but pleasant, and he took a deep breath to calm his nerves and ground himself back in his body. Everything looked different at night, even simple houses lit up by street and porch lights.

"As long as no one sees me out here and calls the cops," he chuckled. Trying to explain why he was out here to the police and Sara at this hour of the morning was not on a list of things he wanted to do.

He looked across the street to the small walkway between the Stevens' home and the empty house that hadn't sold yet. Beyond that was a small field, and then… the woods.

"This is *so* not a good idea," he said, and he felt nerves washing through his stomach again as his heart rate increased. Taking another deep breath in to center himself, he checked the small flashlight on his key chain, and found that the light still worked.

"This is nuts!"

And with those wise words, he walked down his driveway, across the street, and into the passageway leading to the unknown.

• • •

The field was thick with summer grass and foliage and hadn't been cut down for some time. He walked over the uneven ground, trying to keep his tiny flashlight focused on the ground to avoid any nasty surprises, whether flora or fauna. The trees loomed before him now, and while he was apprehensive, there was also an odd calm in the center of his being.

"Whatever's happening, it's supposed to be happening," he said aloud, as much to convince himself of its truth as anything. He took the last few, tentative steps out of the field and stood in front of the first of the trees. They seemed larger, older, more twisted, more imposing at night, but maybe that was just because he rarely came out here at any time. Maples, oaks, birch, maybe others. He knew little about the varieties, but looking into them, he saw only absolute black, a darkness that no moonlight could hope to penetrate.

He turned to gaze back at his neighborhood, which seemed to almost fade away in the dark, becoming a swirl of shapes lost in the murky light of a setting moon. For a moment, he almost thought he was looking at another world, or at least one that was very different than his own.

He shook his head. "Now your imagination's running away with you!"

He turned back to the trees. If anything, the dark was even deeper now. He shone his flashlight into the inky blackness of the tree shadows, but nothing revealed itself. It was like the light simply vanished into the darkness, swallowed up as if by a black hole.

He exhaled sharply.

"Right, I'm doing this! No turning back now," even though every instinct in his body told him to flee from this place, rush back home, and seek safety in his own bed, under the covers, with Sara. His heart rate rose again, and the nerves came back into his stomach with a fury.

But he took a step. And then another. And a third. Twigs and leaves crunched under his feet. The air here smelled damp and musty, forest scents mingling together in an earthy bouquet.

"Well, if you were hoping to do this quietly, that just went out the window," he sighed. "But do what? What am I doing? Where the hell am I even going?"

And there it was again: that lure, that call, like a siren song drawing him into the depths of the unknown. Something tugged at him and beckoned him, even urged him to continue, no matter what his animal instincts and monkey mind might want.

Gripping his flashlight, he took another few steps, trying to keep his breathing steady and let his fear of his surroundings fade away.

"No matter what happens, I have to do this!"

It was an absurd statement. What if he tripped and fell and injured himself? What if something, or someone, attacked him? What about Sara and the kids? What would they think of him creeping around the woods in the early hours of the morning? How would he ever explain it?

A few more steps. And several more. And then he was surrounded by the silent forest on all sides. There were no sounds: no owls hooting, no insects chirping, no small creatures rustling about on the forest floor. It was curious, even unnatural. It sent a shiver down his spine.

His flashlight flickered and went out, leaving him surrounded by darkness.

"Oh, you have *got* to be kidding me! That's it, this is ridiculous. I'm going home."

A light flickered somewhere in the distance, just for a moment. He blinked and squinted, sure that he'd imagined it. As he strained to see into the black, it flickered again, more like at the edge of his awareness than being an actual light he could perceive. Steeling himself, he took a tentative step forward, and then another.

"This is the dumbest thing I've ever done," he said, perhaps a bit louder than he intended. But that volume gave him the confidence he needed, and he began talking as he stepped through the dark.

"I don't know what you are," he said, "but it's clear that you won't leave me alone. How long has this been going on, now? Months? Maybe years? I don't even know. Maybe you've been around my whole life and I'm only remembering it now. But I want some answers. If you're out here and you've been messing with my life, I want to know why. And I want to know who you are."

He had a momentary regret for not bringing his hand gun with him, but that would have required getting into the closet and the locked box on the top shelf.

"And anyway, what would the cops think if they found you wandering around in the woods in the middle of the night, in your sleep clothes and waving a gun around?" He laughed out loud at the thought.

The light flickered again, just at the edge of his vision. Somehow, it was both peripheral and straight ahead at the same time. It made no sense, but neither did being out here.

"I'm here," he said in a louder voice. "I'm doing what you want. This is what you want, right? Hello? I can't see anything, and I really don't want to trip and fall, or get lost. If you're here, show yourself. Hello?"

A glow, both cold and warm, flashed into being before him. Somewhere ahead, in a clearing, something pulsed, its light ebbing and flowing, almost as if it were alive.

"Crap!" A shiver ran down his back, and a momentary surge of fear stopped him in his tracks. "Okay, then, you *are* here."

So startling was this development that the sheer absurdity of the whole situation seemed to simply fall away from him in that moment.

"It's real, it's all real. I haven't been dreaming."

He walked again, this time with more eagerness. He went toward this pulsing light, this living luminance that called to him from this world and maybe the next. As he walked, he felt his senses begin to be dulled, as if he were slipping back into a dream-like state.

"No," he whispered, trying to shake it off.

But it draped over him like a blanket, and whether it was hypnosis, sleep, or some kind of drug, he couldn't fight against it. He felt his body moving, but he no longer seemed to control it. The light loomed ever closer to him, but he had difficulty focusing. Light and dark swirled in front of his eyes, and even when he closed them, the patterns remained. It was as if the source was both in the world and in his mind at the same time. He shook his head to try to clear it, but nothing changed.

"Who… are…"

He felt a soft touch on his arms, slender fingers that seemed to be guiding him. There was a scent of ozone, and even cardboard, as absurd as that seemed. Nothing made sense, nothing could even make sense. The harder he tried to focus, the more everything seemed to be a blur. A second hand took his and he felt its soft but plain skin, dry and cool in one moment and warm in the next.

Words sounded in his mind, or did he hear them? He opened his eyes, or did he close them? He took a few more steps, or was something moving him? He seemed to be floating now, his legs no longer necessary.

He had no choice but to give in, surrender to this presence that called to him, that wanted him, but for what he couldn't know. And then the darkness took him.

. . .

Jace opened his eyes with a start, again tumbling out of sleep. He inhaled sharply and looked around. It was morning, 8:43 to be exact. Sara wasn't next to him. He rubbed his eyes and looked around. The bedroom seemed normal, no sign of anything out of place. Sara must have woken up early (she usually did that, even on weekends) and snuck out to let him sleep in a bit more. He sat up and looked at himself. Nothing out of the ordinary. He sighed.

"Those dreams are getting so crazy! I could've sworn I was up last night."

He let his mind wander over the last few hours. He remembered going downstairs, going outside, walking into the field, and then the forest, and seeing… something? But now, he was just here and he had no memory of coming back home.

"I must have had a dream about waking up and going out," he sighed. "That's nuts!"

He dragged himself out of bed and stood, up, feeling a little wobbly.

"Maybe we shouldn't have had the whole bottle of wine last night," he joked, though he didn't feel hungover or have a headache.

The smell of coffee caught his attention, and he smiled as he stumbled to the bedroom door, left a bit open by Sara. He could hear her downstairs, talking with Grace and Tom. The sounds and the smells brought him into to the moment, out of his head, and back into the real world.

Whatever "real" means.

He descended the stairs and went into the kitchen, where sure enough, his family was situated around the breakfast table in various ways: Tom standing, Grace sitting, and Sara up and down. He smiled. "Hey."

"Hi dad!" Tom said, munching down the last of a waffle held in his hands.

"Hi dad!" Grace said, in between gulps of her orange juice.

Jace smiled at his children, but noted that Sara seemed a little cool.

"So, what are you all up to today?" he asked, looking back and forth between them.

"You are joking, right?' Tom said, giving him the eye.

Jace shook his head. "What?" Sara's glare became more intense.

"It's Saturday," Tom answered, hands held out, palms up, as if this was the most obvious answer in the world.

"I know," Jace said, almost defensively.

"Yeah, and?" Grace butted in.

"Jace," Sara sounded annoyed as she rolled her eyes.

"The school science fair," Tom said, now sounding annoyed, too. "Starting at noon? The one you're helping us with when we set up our booth?"

"Right, of course, I know that!" Jace was embarrassed about his momentary forgetfulness. *Is that today, already?*

"You are going to help us, right?" Grace's tone was almost pouty, almost guilt-tripping, but Jace couldn't blame her. He knew he was on the edge of majorly screwing this up, hence Sara's stares.

"Absolutely! I will. I'll be there. I will!"

Grace and Tom look relieved and both smiled.

"Great," said Tom. "Just make sure you're there an hour before it opens. We still have a lot to do. Phil's mom is stopping by in a few minutes to give us a ride to the hall."

"Excellent," said Jace, smiling at them both. "I promise I'll be there on time. I wouldn't miss it!"

To a chorus of "Thanks dad!" Tom and Grace ran out of the kitchen and scurried upstairs to get ready. And still Sara was giving him the look.

"You forgot, didn't you?" she said after their kids were out of earshot.

"No, I did not. I'm just tired, a lot on my mind lately. You know that."

"That's becoming your pat answer to everything."

"Look, Sara, I'm sorry. I know this is an important day for them. They've worked hard on their environmental display. I'll be there, I promise you and them."

"Make sure you are," she turned away and put milk and orange juice back in the fridge.

"Am I getting the literal cold shoulder now?" he tried to joke, but regretted his words at once.

Sara froze. "Jace…"

"Look," he said, "I'm sorry, really. Things have been tense at work these past few weeks, and… and I'm having those dreams, more and more often. Like, every night now. They happened again last night, really vivid this time. One was so real, I thought I actually woke up. I saw you sleeping and went to the window. The moon was over the woods, and I just, I don't know, felt like I needed to walk out to them for some reason. It's crazy, I know. So I did. Walk out to the forest, I mean. I got my flashlight and marched across the field and went into those damned trees. But then, my flashlight gave out and something was there, in the dark, calling to me. I felt like I couldn't control myself, like I was floating or something. And then I blacked out, and then I woke up, and here I am."

Sara sighed. "This is getting worse. I don't think it's just work stress."

"Well, you're the shrink. If you have any ideas, I'm open to suggestion."

"You know I can't treat you. It's unethical to work on family members, except in emergencies."

"I'd say this is starting to feel like an emergency to me. So, am I nuts?"

"No, you're not nuts…" Sara lowered her voice as Grace and Tom bounded down the stairs and out the door.

"Bye mom, bye dad!"

"Bye guys, have a great day, and I *will* be there!" Jace called out after them.

"But I think you're under a lot of pressure," Sara continued once they were gone. "Probably way more than even you know. And everybody has different ways of reacting to it, ways that sometimes even surprise them."

Jace rubbed his face as he poured himself some coffee. "Maybe, but why now? It's been a bit rough lately, but not that much rougher. I mean, I've had these dreams in the past, but it's like, lately, they come every night. I'm getting to where I'm afraid to go to sleep, because I don't want to deal with them. I wake up feeling more tired than when I went to bed."

"I think your unconscious mind might be trying to tell you something."

"Is that an official, unethical diagnosis?" he grinned.

Sara smiled a little. "No, it's the words of a concerned wife who loves you and wants you to feel better."

Tom took a large gulp of coffee. "So, what should I do, oh wise one?"

"I can't treat you, but I can refer you. I'd like you to meet with my colleague, Cassandra Hill. She's a great therapist who…"

"Sara…" Jace groaned and rolled his eyes.

"No, I'm serious, Jace! You have to get on top of this. You can't keep going on, night after night, tossing and turning, having bizarre dreams, and waking up exhausted. It's stressing you out, it's stressing *me* out, and we need to figure out what's going on."

Jace sighed and put down his mug. "Fine. What does she do?"

"She's really good at hypnotherapy."

"Wait, she's a hypnotist? Is she going to make me think I'm a dog, or something?"

"No, you jerk! A hypnotherapist. It's a valid, well-documented tool for helping people get to the bottom of their problems. It's a way of relaxing you, so that your conscious mind doesn't interfere with memories and feelings that it might be trying to suppress. If your dreams are being caused by stress or trauma, you might just be able to figure out what that cause is, and then she can help treat it. She's had great success with a lot of people in the past."

Jace looked down for a moment, trying to think of something he could say to argue against the idea, but he came up blank. He sighed again.

"Okay, fine. I'll do it. For you."

"Don't just do it for me, do it for yourself." She came over and gave him a hug, which oddly, was the most welcome thing she could offer him in that moment. He savored her warmth, her feel. It was grounding, and for the first time since he'd woken up, he felt like himself again.

"Thank you," she said, parting from him, but keeping her arms draped over his shoulders. "We need to get to the bottom of this, and I think she'll really help."

"Fair enough. I'll go get myself hypnotized."

"Good. I'll phone her today and reserve a spot for you this week," Sara said, stepping back. "She's a friend, so I can ask a favor and get you in with a short-order appointment."

"Honestly, the sooner the better. I'd like this to go away, to be honest."

"You and me both." She grabbed a couple of plates and walked back over to the sink to rinse them.

"Oh, one other thing," she said, turning and looking back at him. "I promise I'm not trying to nag, but can you not leave your shoes in the living room and your keys on the dining table? We're trying to set a good example for the kids, and they 'forget' enough about it as it is. Everything stays by the door, remember?"

"What?" A shock ran through him like an electrical volt.

Sara turned. "Your shoes and your keys? You left them in the living room? We're trying not to do that?"

"No, wait, no…" Jace dashed off into the living room. Sure enough, his shoes were on the carpet, looking as if they'd been kicked off in a hurry. An inspection of the dining room table revealed his keys were indeed there, also set down in a haphazard way.

"This is, this is impossible," he stammered, stunned and not sure what to believe.

"Jace… what is it?" Sara came up behind him and put a hand on his shoulder. She sounded worried.

"My shoes," he said. "They were right by the door last night, on the shoe rack. I swear! So were my keys, hanging on the key hook. I know for a fact they were because I remember setting them there. There's no way they could be in here."

"But why would anyone move them?"

"I don't know." He turned to Sara. "Look, I promise you, my shoes and keys were by the door last night. I saw them when I checked to make sure that both locks were set on the door before we went to bed. I check the door every night, just to be sure."

"Jace, you're scaring me. What are you saying?"

"Well, since it's unlikely the kids got up and moved them in the middle of the night, I must have done it myself. It's the only explanation."

"And you don't remember doing it?"

"Maybe I'm sleep-walking." A chill went down his back and he stared at her in alarm. "Maybe I really *did* go out into the woods last night!"

CHAPTER 2

"MS. HILL?

"Call me Cassandra,"

She offered her hand and Jace shook it.

"Thanks for meeting me on such short notice." He looked around the room, and was pleased that it didn't resemble a "typical" therapist's office, whatever that was.

"Not a problem. I had a cancellation this week, and was glad I could fit you in."

He looked at her again. "Have we met before?"

She shook her head. "I don't think so. I mean, I've known Sara as a colleague for ages, but I don't think you and I have ever met."

"Hm, probably not, you just look a bit familiar." Unable to place where he might have seen her, he sat himself down on the couch opposite of her chair.

"Maybe I just have one of 'those' faces," she smiled.

"Yeah. So…"

"So, you've read all the introductory materials?"

"I have," he nodded.

"And I've read about you based on your questionnaire." She sat down with a note pad. "Is there anything else you'd like to tell me before we start?"

"We're just going to start? Like, right now?"

She nodded. "Unless you have anything else you feel you need to talk about first."

He sighed and slumped farther back into the couch. "Not really. I just assumed you'd want to talk to me about everything before we started. You know, my relationship with my mother, that sort of thing."

She chuckled. "This is a different kind of therapy. The point here is to let you explore what's on your mind, and then we can talk about it afterward."

"Ah, so I get to pick what I want to talk about, based on what comes up when I'm under?"

"Something like that. It also gives me a chance to observe you in an unbiased way. I haven't formed any opinions yet, so you won't feel like I'm judging you, or expecting you to come up with certain answers, or things that I want to hear."

"Fair enough. Do I need to lie down?"

"Sitting comfortably is fine. That's why I have such a nice couch!"

"Yeah, it's a good one; I could go to sleep on it."

"That happens sometimes."

"What, you mean people fall asleep in the middle of a session?"

"If they're relaxed enough."

"Okay, well I'll try not to."

"No pressure and no expectations, remember? We're here to explore."

"Got it. So what do I do?"

"Sit comfortably and close your eyes. I'm going to guide you through some visualizations and then count down to a point where you're very relaxed."

"And that's it?"

She grinned. "I'm not going to pull out a pocket watch and tell you you're getting sleepy, if that's what you mean!"

Jace chuckled. He was beginning to like her, in spite of his reservations about coming here, about trying this.

"Now close your eyes, and take three deep, calming breaths."

He let her guide him through a series of visualizations, which he was happy to discover were not as strange or "New Age" as he'd feared. Then came the countdown from ten to one.

When she'd finished, he heard her say in a calm voice, "Let your mind wander now, and let's see what it wants to come up with. You've been having disturbing dreams lately. Can you find anything that might be useful in understanding more about them? If not, that's fine. Remember, we're here to explore. Tell me if you see anything, but don't try to make images come to your mind. Just let them happen as they come up."

Jace sat in silence for a few moments. *Nothing but black*, he thought. Or did he? Was he actually under? Was he hypnotized? He felt like he could open his eyes at any moment, but for whatever reason, he didn't want to. It felt good being here, even if nothing came to mind.

"I'm not really seeing anything…"

"Just relax and let whatever comes to you happen in its own time."

He felt his head nod forward just a little. *Great, am I gonna fall asleep and make a fool out myself in the first session?*

But he felt something begin to come to mind: only a sensation at first, but then a vision, faint and just at the edge of awareness. Was it a memory?

"I think… I feel like… something is there. I mean, no, I mean, I'm there… somewhere. I feel like I'm remembering something? I don't know. It might just be a load of crap."

"Relax, breath evenly, and let it come."

"I think I'm in a bed. My bed, I mean. But not mine. No, I mean not mine right now. I think, I think it's my bed from when I was a kid, but here I'm like, maybe fifteen or something? I have no idea why I'm getting this!"

"Just let it happen."

"It's night, but it's bright outside. Outside my window, I mean. The moon, probably, shining in through the window. But it's too bright. The moon isn't that bright. It's weird. I'm awake, but I'm also asleep, I think. That makes no sense. Something… something's there."

"In the room?"

"No, at the window. Something's looking in. It's an owl? Yeah, an owl. A big owl. Just looking at me."

"It's sitting on the window ledge looking at you?"

"Yeah, but that's the weird thing. That window, it doesn't have a ledge. So there's, there's an owl, but it's not flying, it's just, I don't know, hovering, but not moving. That makes no sense at all!"

"It doesn't have to make sense. Just let it be what it wants to. Is the owl doing anything?"

"Okay, this is crazy, but I think it's trying to talk to me. Not talk, really, but *think* at me. Like somehow, I can hear what it's saying, but in my head, only in my head."

"And what is it saying?"

"I'm not sure. It's a language of some kind, but I don't understand it. Not one word. If it's trying to talk to me, it's not doing a very good job."

"Why do you think it's trying to talk to you?"

"I don't know."

"How do you feel about it being there?"

"I mean, I should be scared, right? I should be freaked out that there's this huge owl looking at me, trying to read my mind or something, but I'm not really scared. I feel like I know it somehow, even if I can't understand it."

"Is the owl your friend?"

"I'm not sure 'friend' is the right word. But I feel like it knows me and it's, I don't know, looking out for me, somehow?"

"What does the owl look like?"

"Like a big barn owl, you know, the ones with the white faces. But this one, the eyes. They're different somehow. They're darker, like jet black, and larger too, bigger than a typical owl. It's like those eyes see things. They know things."

"What do they know?"

"Not sure. Things it hasn't told me yet. Probably because I don't understand it!" He chuckled.

"Is there anything else happening?"

"Not that I can tell."

"How long does this owl stay there?"

"For a while. I don't know, like twenty minutes, or something? Then it just kind of drifts away, back into the light in the distance, back to the moon, I guess. But it can't really be the moon. I'm alone again."

"How do you feel?"

"Weirdly calm. I should be freaking the hell out, but I'm not."

"Do you know if the owl has come to your window before?"

"I think so, but I'm not sure. Like I said, I feel like I know it, so it must have been by before, right?"

"Is there anything else, you want to tell me about this night? Do you know if it happens again?"

"I feel like it does, later on. Maybe every few months or something. I get the impression that I knew this was happening when I was a teenager, but then I just kind of forgot about it later, you know?"

"All right, let's move on from that. I want you to take three deep breaths and clear your mind of those images. Open up to being blank again."

Jace did as she asked and found himself feeling even more relaxed, sinking farther into the couch. He again feared he was going to nod off at any minute.

"Would you like to explore the dreams you've been having recently?"

"Yeah, yeah, sure."

"Okay then, calm yourself and again, let whatever comes to your mind just pop in there. I want you to focus on your recent dreams and see what could show up as a clue to what they might mean. But remember, don't force it, just let it happen."

"Okay, okay, got it."

He felt a sense of unease creeping over him. "I'm getting kind of tense, sorry."

"Do you know why?"

"No, it's just that these dreams don't seem as calm as the owl dream, or whatever it was."

"Stay with it, take three more deep breaths and clear your head."

Jace did as she asked and found that he started to calm down again.

"Can you remember when these dreams started?" he heard her ask.

"Three or four months ago, maybe? I don't know. I think I'd had them before, but like I said, I just, just put them out of my mind, or forgot about them… something."

"And now?"

"Now, I think they're happening most nights, even if I don't always remember them."

"What usually happens?"

"I'm in my room, my bedroom *now*, that is. Sara's, she's sleeping next to me. There's a light again, outside, outside the window. I think it's the moon, but the moon can't be that bright every night, right? It waxes and wanes. But this light, it's always the same. There's nothing there, by the way, nothing outside the window. No owl. Just the light. But someone's with me."

"Someone?"

"Yeah, I don't know who it is. I can't see them well, at all. But I get a sense that there's someone standing nearby, on my side of the bed."

"What are they doing?"

"Watching. Observing. That seems to be all, really."

"How do you feel?"

"Tense. Afraid. Maybe not terrified, but it feels weird, you know? Having someone in my house, in my bedroom, just watching me. I don't like it. But I don't feel like whoever it is wants to hurt me, or Sara. I don't know, it's just a feeling I get. I might be wrong."

"What does this person do?"

"Nothing, that's the whole weirdness of it. They're just watching. And then, they leave, going back to the light, like the owl did."

"Where do they go?"

"Out the window, I guess, but I don't see it, see them leave. It's like they're here in one minute and then gone in the next, but I don't see them come or go."

"What happens next?"

"I go back to sleep, I guess. Sara never even wakes up. This is only for me, only for me to see."

"Did they tell you that?"

"No, but that's what it feels like."

"Does anything else happen?"

"No, I think… I think this goes on most nights, maybe not every night. But whoever it is, they're visiting me a lot."

"Do they say anything to you?"

"You mean like in some weird owl language? No, not that I can tell."

"Is there anything else you want to explore while you're here?"

"Not really I mean… well, there's this desire I have. Something I want to do, I *need* to do."

"Tell me about it."

"I need to go into the forest. To Fairburn Woods, near our house. Something's out there."

"What is it?"

"I don't know, but I need to get out there. At night, I mean. And I think I did, over this past weekend."

"You went into the woods?"

"I think so. I must have been sleepwalking, but now it feels like I was awake at the time, even if I couldn't remember what happened the next morning."

"Can you go there now? Can you tell me what you saw out there?"

Jace grimaced. "I want to, but I feel like I can't. Not yet. When I try to let it come to me, you know, like you said, it's like there's a wall there, and I can't climb over it. It's like something doesn't want me to know what happened. Not yet, anyway."

"All right Jace, that's enough for now. Take three deep breaths and I'll count you back up."

Jace did as she asked and let her guide him back to the waking world over the next several minutes.

"Wow," he said, looking around and patting himself down to ground himself. "That was wild!"

"Lots of things can come up when the mind is relaxed enough to let them in."

"And that was it?" He still couldn't believe it. "I was really hypnotized?"

"You were," she said with a smile.

"How did I do?"

"It's not about *doing* anything. It's not about a score. It's about exploring and seeing what your unconscious mind wants to tell you."

"Seems like it told me a lot! So what does it all mean?"

"That's what we're going to find out. But don't try to assign too much meaning to anything, not yet. It will take a while to figure out what your mind is trying to tell you."

"You mean we have to do this again?"

She chuckled. "It's not a one-and-done treatment, I'm afraid."

He sighed. "All right, fine. I'll come back for more. In the meantime, should I talk about this with Sara?"

Cassandra shrugged. "That's up to you. If you think it would help, then by all means, do it. Maybe she'll have some perspectives on things that you're not thinking about."

He shook his head. "This is going to make for some interesting bed-time conversation!"

• • •

"So, you saw something… looking at you? An owl?" Sara looked at Jace with suspicion. He'd waited until they were in bed and the kids were asleep to reveal the session's surprising results to her. Her reaction was pretty much what he expected.

"I think so," he sighed. "I don't know what it meant, but when I was… under, I guess, it all seemed really real. Like it wasn't my imagination, but actual memories that I've shut away, or maybe that were shut away for me."

"What does that mean?"

"I don't know. I don't even know what I'm saying, but I got the sense that, that something's been happening to me, but my mind, my conscious mind, I guess… it won't let me remember, at least not right now. Or maybe something's stopping me from remembering. I don't know."

"You realize that does sound pretty…"

"Crazy? Yeah, thanks, I know."

"Jace, I didn't mean…"

"No, but you're thinking it, right? Like something's really wrong with me? I'm going nuts?"

"No! I just think that you're under a lot of stress and you're tired, and all of this is building up and it's coming out of you in weird ways."

"Maybe, but what about that first memory? The owl, when I was a teenager? How am I making that up now? Why did that come back, if it even came back?"

She sighed and closed her eyes. "I don't know. Jace… you don't think…"

"What?"

"This is going to sound awful, but I'm going to say it, anyway: you don't think you were abused as a child or a teenager, do you? That something happened and you shut it out?"

"No! God, no, Sara! How could you think that? You know my parents, they're amazing! No, no, if something like that had happened, I'd know, I'd remember."

"But would you? Our minds can do incredible things to protect us from thoughts and memories that we can't face up to."

"So I should do, what? Accuse my dad of hitting me? Molesting me? God, Sara, what are you even thinking?"

"I'm not accusing him, and you shouldn't, either." She put a hand on his shoulder. "I'm just saying that it sounds like your unconscious mind is really stressed about something right now, and it's trying to come out. I want you to be ready for it, whatever it is, because it might be something you won't like. I mean, come on, if you think you're sleepwalking out in Fairburn, that's dangerous! You could trip and hurt yourself, or get attacked."

"By what? The wild wolves of the woods? There's nothing out there, Sara."

"Well, if you're going out there, you must think there is."

"Maybe, I don't know. Look, I'm feeling overwhelmed by this, and I'm tired. I just want to try to get some sleep."

Sara didn't say anything else but turned the light out and rolled over. He wasn't happy with this, not the dreams, not the tension between them, none of it. He took a couple of deep breaths and tried to calm himself, as he'd done in Dr. Hill's office.

Maybe I can do it to myself—hypnosis—and find out more. And that's completely ridiculous. I'll probably just make something up.

Still, he closed his eyes and tried to imagine himself sitting on Cassandra's couch again. If there was any chance he could bring himself back to that state...

His mind wandered, but he felt an unusual wave of fatigue slipping over him. Too much had happened, and though he wanted to stay awake and try to explore the deeper recesses of his mind, his body fought against him. He gave in and fell into a deep, dreamless sleep.

. . .

Jace opened his eyes with a start. It was still dark. He wanted to glance at the clock, but he already knew what time it was: 3:33 am. He tried to turn his head, just to confirm, but he found he couldn't move. Neck, arms, hands, legs, feet... nothing. He was paralyzed. A panic washed over him and he tried to call out, but he couldn't even make a sound.

He felt his heart beat faster and heavier as he opened his eyes wide, straining to look around him in every direction, as much as he could. His breathing was shallow and rapid and he could feel a trickle of sweat fall down the right side of his head.

Something's here.

The words came to his mind, but did he think them, or were they placed there? Straining to glance as far to the right as possible, he was aware of a shape, a figure of some sort standing in the shadows. More than one, maybe? It wasn't tall, it wasn't imposing, but it was there.

Something's here!

He wanted to shout to scream, to wake up Sara and tell her to run, but nothing escaped from him. The silence of the room was overwhelming. If the beings nearby breathed, he couldn't hear them.

Okay, all right, calm down, Jace. This is a nightmare. You're dreaming. This is that sleep paralysis thing you've read about. It's not really happening, your mind has gone into overdrive and it's making you think you're stuck, but you're not! You can wake up from this. Come on! Do it!

He was aware of movement to his right. A being, a shadow, something was approaching him.

Come on, damn it! Wake up!

His breathing rapid, he again tried to get a look at whatever was now looming over him. It seemed oddly small and slender, almost like a child. He had a thought that maybe Grace or Tom had come into the room, but that made no sense, and in any case, they were both bigger than this figure.

He tried to open his mouth, tried to speak, but words failed.

What are you? What do you want? Maybe he could think thoughts at it.

We are you. We need what you have.

The sound of a disembodied voice in his mind stunned him. It was odd, cold, even mechanical in tone, but it was undeniably not his imagination.

What are you talking about? I don't have anything! You have no right to be here, in my home!

The shadow seemed to incline forward just a little. *We have every right.*

The words struck Jace like a punch in the stomach. What did they mean? *I don't understand, I...*

He felt a sharp pinch in his right ear, followed by a burning sensation. He wanted to grunt in pain, but again, no sounds could escape him.

What's happening? What are you doing?

The shadow seemed to float back a bit from him. *It is accomplished. And soon you must begin.*

Jace's fury at this intrusion, this violation, was almost uncontrollable. If he could have, he would have leaped out of bed that very moment and punched whoever was there. But again, he was held fast in place. *Begin, begin what?*

To save a world...

. . .

The alarm went off, but he barely heard it. It was only when Sara started shaking him with some vigor that he roused enough to open his eyes and roll over.

Roll over!

He could move! He remembered something about not being able to do so last night, of being held in place while someone, something, stood over him. Did something to him.

"Jace, come on! The alarm's already gone off twice now." Sara nudged him again.

He sighed. "Ugh, I don't feel all that well. I might have to give everything a miss today."

"Well, if you're going to call in sick, you'd better let them know soon." Sara got up and left the room without saying anything else. She still seemed mad.

He stared after her, a mix of emotions surging through him. He understood why she was so uneasy, but he was also annoyed that she didn't seem to be listening to him. She was the one who'd suggested Cassandra Hill, after all, practically shoved him into it. And now, she didn't like the results?

"Not my problem," he said with a groan as he noticed an ache in his right ear. He reached up to touch it, and it felt sensitive.

"What the hell?"

He felt around the earlobe and the top part, but nothing seemed unusual. He couldn't find the exact place where the pain was located; it just ached all over, almost like he'd been punched.

"Great, am I sleep-fighting now, too?"

He thought about getting up, pushing through it, and getting ready for work, like any other day. But something about today felt different. Something had changed.

"And that makes no sense at all," he said.

"What makes no sense?" Grace popped her head around the door.

"Oh, nothing, just the world in general," Jace said with a smile. "How's it going, Gracie?"

"I'm fine. Mom said you're not feeling well, that you're going to stay home today?"

"Thinking about it."

"Okay, cool." She came in and gave him a kiss on the cheek. "Well, feel better soon. I have to get ready."

"I will. Thanks, honey."

As she left, he remembered something. There had been someone standing over him last night, or at least, he dreamed there was.

"At the time, I think I thought that it was too short to be Grace. I was right! Looking at her now, there's no way that was her, never mind Tom. But why would I think that in a dream? Why would it even matter? Gah, I'm pretty sure I'm cracking up!"

He sat up in bed, thrilled simply to be able to move.

"Sleep paralysis is awful!"

He swung himself to the side of the bed, and sat there for a moment, trying to get his bearings and process whatever this latest dream might mean. A wave of dizziness washed over him and he had to lie back down.

"What the hell? Oh, damn, I think I really am sick!"

He kept his head down for some time, until the spinning had passed. Sara came back in.

"How are you feeling?' Her tone was oddly cold and uncaring.

"Not too good, I think I really do need to stay home today."

"Have you called it in?"

"Texting my team right now." He grabbed his phone from the night stand and sent a message. "Done. Now, I think I'm going to go back to sleep."

"Okay. Feel better, I'll see you tonight." She grabbed a set of clothes from the dresser and closet and left the bedroom without saying another word.

Jace blew out a sharp puff of air. *Why is she so upset about this? I'm the one going through it! You know, a little love and understanding here would be nice!*

He closed his eyes and tried to think again about last night's dream. Nothing made sense.

Why is this happening? What's really going on? Am I hiding something from myself?

He turned his head to the right and happened to glance down at his pillow. He was struck by what he saw and sat upright in an instant. There, on the pillow case, near where his right ear would be as he slept, was a single drop of dried blood.

CHAPTER 3

"SO, YOU HAVEN'T TOLD HER?" Cassandra looked at Jace with concern.

Jace shook his head. "I didn't want to worry her yet, not until I can figure out a bit more about what's going on."

"But you think you might have hurt yourself in your sleep, or in some kind of hypnogogic state."

"To be honest, I don't know what I think. It's all so crazy. What do you think?"

"I think you're undergoing some kind of traumatic event. It might be triggered by what's happening in your life right now, or it might be bubbling up from your unconscious, in reaction to memories from some time ago."

"Sara asked me if I thought I might have been abused as a child."

"What do you think?"

"I don't... honestly? I don't think so. Really, I'm not just saying that because I think that's what you want to hear. I just don't see how it's possible. There would have been something, a memory, a sign, *something* if anything like that had happened, and I'm sure it didn't."

"So, what do you think it really is, then?"

"You're not helping here, you know," he chuckled.

"I'm trying to get you to focus on what's best for you. The last thing I want to do is go putting suggestions into your mind about the cause of your stress. It's much better if you can come to that on your own."

"I know," he nodded. "So, can we try to figure out what happened the other night?"

"If that's what you'd like to focus on, then yes, absolutely."

"Great, thanks. Okay, do your magic, then."

It was Cassandra's turn to chuckle as she led him through the hypnosis exercises and once more into a deeply relaxed state. Jace found that he was calmer sitting here on this couch than he was in his own home. This was a good place, and a good state of mind to be in. That was something, at least.

"Now," she said in a soothing voice, "let's take a look at what might have happened the other night. Can you bring yourself back to your bedroom, to that time?"

Jace nodded, his eyes closed. "Yeah, yeah, it's easier this time than before. I must be getting better at this. Okay, so… I'm in my bed, I'm awake, but I'm paralyzed, I can't move at all, can't even turn my head."

"Are you alone?"

"No, no. Sara is sleeping next to me, out like a light, as usual. I can just see her."

"What else can you see?"

"It's dark, but not too dark." Jace moved his head back and forth, as if that would somehow help him see more of what was happening in his mind's eye. "There's that light outside the window, the one from before, when the owl was there, you know, when I was younger. But the owl, it's not there. There's something else though, next to me, on my right."

"Who is it?"

"More like *what* is it, I think. It's weird; it's small but huge somehow. I know that makes no sense. Huge in the sense of a big presence, I think. Like, it has a big mind. That's just stupid."

"Remember, say whatever you feel comfortable saying."

"Yeah, yeah, got it. I can't turn my head to see it, but it's there, and it's saying something to me, in my mind. Not out loud. But still, words."

"Try to expand your mind, try to take in more of the scene. It might be only in your peripheral vision, but maybe you can still recall what it looks like?"

Jace winced. "I'm trying, I think you're right. I think I can see it, I just blocked it from my memory, or maybe *they* did, I don't know. But yeah, I think I can expand my vision, I can… holy sh…"

"What do you see?"

"It's so bizarre! There's a little being, thin, spindly, even; thin arms and legs. It's got a big head, though, with large almond-shaped eyes. They're totally black. I don't see a nose, or even much of a mouth. It's like one of those aliens you see on tabloids, or something. This is nuts! It's watching me, it and another one behind it. It's speaking to me, saying things, something about saving the Earth, or something. I don't know; it doesn't make sense."

"Does it do anything else?"

"Yeah, yeah, now I can see it. It's reaching for my ear, my right one. It says it needs to put something in me, something that will help me to help them, and remember. Remember what? It's going to also help me traverse time… what does that even mean? I feel something, like a burning in my ear, yeah, it's hot! And then, then it's like a poke, a prick on the skin somewhere, like from a needle, but the needle is really hot. It's like it's piercing my ear, or something. And the voice says it might be a day or two before it takes effect. I don't know what that means. And then they say other things, about saving the Earth again, and then they're gone and I'm out cold, like the deepest sleep I've had in ages. Oh man, I'm going nuts."

"Let's end there and bring you out."

Cassandra guided Jace back into waking consciousness, but even after he opened his eyes, he still felt disconnected, as if he was somewhere else. He closed his eyes again, as if hoping he could be back in that memory, but no new images came to mind. Opening them, he stared across at Cassandra, but couldn't gauge her reaction, or what she thought of it all. It was kind of infuriating, but at least she was good at her job.

"So, am I crazy? Seeing little green men in my bedroom?" He smiled, but it felt insincere.

"No, Jace, you're not, and we don't use words like that, not in my office, anyway. I do think that you're under severe stress, and you're using these images as a coping mechanism to hide something that you might not be able to face yet."

"But what about the little being? The alien thing?"

"It's a common enough image in pop culture; you might have just grabbed onto it because it came to mind."

"But why would I? I'm not even interested in that, except, you know, watching the occasional sci-fi show or movie."

"We can't always explain why our minds do what they do. Maybe that image is comforting to you for reasons that you don't even know about yet."

He sighed. "It's all crazy. Sorry, I didn't mean…"

"It's fine." she shook her head with a slight smile. "But I think you and Sara need to talk about this and really try to get to the bottom of what's going on. I'm concerned that if you don't, it's only going to get worse and more intense."

"I will," he sighed. But he also knew that there was more to this than just hiding from unpleasant memories. *And I'm going to figure out what it is.*

• • •

He was home before everyone else. Good. Jace stood at the front doorway and glanced around.

"What am I even looking for?"

Everything was where it should be. He had no memories of further early-morning trips into the woods, so his shoes and keys were right where they should be that morning. He walked through the kitchen and looked out into the back yard. Aside from a few untended rose bushes, everything seemed entirely normal.

"If someone's coming and going, it's not through here."

He sighed. Resigning himself once more to putting it down to his imagination, he decided to go up to the bedroom. Stepping over to the window, he checked it.

"Locked, what a surprise," he chuckled. As if something was coming through the window without opening it, making noise, or being seen!

"This is stupid, Jace! There was no one here. There are no little green men, or grey men—whatever. You're under stress, you saw a picture on the cover of a tabloid, or something, and your overactive imagination is playing up. First it was owls, now it's aliens. Cassandra's right. It's probably sleep paralysis, and you're just trying to make it into something weird or fantastic. Face it, you're overworked, exhausted, you can't concentrate on anything, and it's bothering everyone else, especially Sara and the kids. You've got to start reining it in. Work less, relax more, take days off instead of pushing through. To hell with their deadlines. "

He sighed and turned away from the window to leave the room. Out of the corner of his eye he noticed something in the far corner, on his side of the bed.

"What?"

He shook his head and squinted. There were markings on the floor. His heart raced and he approached with caution. Kneeling down, he looked at the carpet, not right beside the bed, but a few feet away. He could see two clear depressions, as if made by small feet.

"These are way too small to be Grace or Tom."

Running his fingers over them he had an odd sensation. Not quite an electric shock, but something unusual, as if emanating from the "footprints" themselves. On instinct, he held up his fingers to his nose. There was a faint smell, like mushrooms or earth, and cardboard. It was the same smell he's sensed in…

"The woods!"

He looked up with a start. Darting his glance around, maybe in hopes of seeing anything else, his mind reeled.

"Something *was* here. Damn it! And something was out there, in those woods. It called to me. They did, whoever."

He tried to stand up, but felt light-headed, and almost fell over. Sitting himself back down on the floor, he tried to make sense of everything.

Something here, in the dark, doing something next to me. Something, or more than one of them, standing by my bed, leaving a trace, some footprints.

"Did they do it on purpose?" he asked aloud. "Was I supposed to see this? Why were they here? What did they do?"

Almost casually, he rubbed his right ear with one hand. And the memory flooded back to him.

"Something about my ear. One of them… one of them did something. They did, it hurt, what?" He felt along his whole ear, trying to dislodge any repressed memories through the sense of touch. He remembered burning, pain. It was brief, but it was real. He felt down to the lobe and his hand ran across…

"What's that?"

Ignoring his dizziness, he stood up and rushed to the bathroom, turning his head in every direction to try to get a better view of his ear. He poked and prodded with both hands now, fingers tracing the whole surface. After a few more seconds of searching, his fingers found something. It was faint, but it was there. A small bump, so small that it seemed to be there one moment and gone the next. He tried holding his fingers in place to see if he could feel it changing size. There was no doubt that it felt stronger and weaker in alternation, like it was pulsing.

"But what the hell is it?"

He tried squeezing both sides of his ear lobe, pressing harder and harder. The pulsing seemed to stop, but he felt no pain. Letting go of the pressure the sensation returned. But as soon as he removed his fingers, it was as if it were not there at all.

"This… this can't be happening. Did those… things put something in my ear? Why?"

Light-headedness overcame him again and he stumbled back into the bedroom, lying down and trying to get his bearings, trying to focus.

"Okay, all right. Use some of that breathing technique stuff that Cassandra uses on you. That'll help. That'll relax you."

Taking three deep breaths in a row, he closed his eyes and tried to let his mind wander, tried not to let these revelations interfere with keeping his thoughts blank for whatever might come up. In his mind's eye, he could only see the black in front of him.

Good, good, he thought. *Let it come. Just let it come.*

His hope for a clear vision of his mysterious intruders did not materialize, and after some time, he resigned himself to once again getting no real answers. He let out a breath and prepared to bring himself back into waking consciousness using Cassandra's methods.

But he felt something, just a faint sense, pulling at him, not letting him go, as if it didn't want him to leave yet. Was he being called? Summoned?

A sound, a voice, came to his mind. It seemed to say something, over and over, in a faint, almost robotic voice. He heard it only in his mind, only in this dark place. Taking another breath, he tried to focus on it, to bring it into his awareness so that he could understand, so that he could know.

A single word in a strange, almost metallic, voice formed in his mind: "Tonight."

• • •

"So how did it go today? You didn't say anything about it earlier." Sara sat with Jace on the couch. It was late, the kids were asleep, and though they'd finished watching a show, his mind was elsewhere.

"Hm? Oh good, really good, actually. She thinks it might be sleep paralysis brought on by stress. Too many hours at work, too much throwing myself into projects and not delegating tasks to others. She thinks I need to really be okay with letting go. Take up some meditation practices. We've been working on some, actually, to supplement her hypnotherapy." That wasn't exactly true, and Jace didn't like lying to her, but tonight was important. Somehow, he just knew it.

"In fact, I think I'm gonna stay up for a bit, and work on one of the techniques. It's a breathing exercise, and I think I'll do better if I'm sitting up, like when I'm at her office. I don't want to disturb you, so go on to bed. I'll be up later. No need to wait up for me. Really, get some sleep. I'll be quiet when I'm done."

Sara looked skeptical for a moment, but then took his hand. "Jace, I just want you to be better. You *would* tell me if anything was really wrong, wouldn't you?"

There was a look of hurt in her eyes, maybe even some fear. It tugged at him, and he had the thought that he should tell her everything. But that passed. He knew he couldn't, not just yet. He had to try to reach out, to make contact, if that was even possible.

"Of course I would," he white-lied, "and if anything changes, you'll be the first to know." *And you will, I promise. As soon as I know what the hell is going on.*

She seemed satisfied with his answer. Giving him a faint smile, she kissed his cheek and got up. "Well, happy meditating. I hope it helps. I'll see you in the morning?"

"Absolutely, and again, Sara, I'm sorry if I've been such a pill lately. It's not you, it's not the kids. I'm just overworked and I have to cut back. I really think that's the key. It's finally dawning on me."

She nodded and with another smile, she turned and went upstairs.

Jace gave a sigh of relief that she'd let him have this time to himself.

"Tonight, I'm gonna figure this out," he whispered. "I'm not putting up with this anymore."

He waited for a while, until he was sure she'd gone to bed. He took a deep breath and settled in comfortably to the couch, just as he'd been doing with Cassandra's help.

"Okay, I'm ready. You said 'tonight,' so show me what you've got. I'm ready, and even if I'm not, I have to be, right? You said so!"

He closed his eyes and set about putting himself into the relaxed state he'd been practicing for the past several days. There was a sense of calm, of peace, that he was pleased to feel coming over him.

Maybe I'm starting to get good at this. Not bad for only a few tries.

But despite his focus, no answers came, no visions, no voices. He found himself growing impatient, which was the last thing he needed as he was trying to put himself into a state of deep relaxation. As he focused, two words came into his mind.

Ona, cam…

Over and over, these words repeated, as if being sent to him, rather than arising from his own mind.

"What's this? Are they words? What language?"

Ona, cam, ona, cam…

He tried to bring his focus to them, reciting them in a whisper as if they were a mantra. Maybe they were the key to unlocking something he'd forgotten? He tried to make them his sole focus, but soon found that instead, he was getting more and more drowsy; it was almost like he'd taken a sleeping pill.

"What's happening?" he whispered. "This is ridiculous! I haven't taken anything to sleep. I haven't…"

The urge to lie down overcame him, and he was only barely aware of slumping over on to the couch, and falling into a deep, dreamless sleep.

. . .

Jace opened his eyes with a start. He was still on the living room couch, where he'd tumbled over. It was dark and quiet, but he knew exactly what time it was without even looking at the clock on the mantle.

He smiled knowingly. "So, this is how it's going to be, eh? Fine. I'm awake, I'm ready, let's do this!" He rubbed his hands over his face with vigor, to make sure that he really was awake.

He knew right away that he had to go to the woods again. Whoever was out there, they were calling to him, they were summoning him, they were waiting.

"At least I can sneak out without disturbing anyone this time. And get back… if I ever come back." The thought struck him as oddly dark, but he had to admit in the moment that he had no idea what was about to happen, only that he had to face it.

Shaking off any doubts, he put on his coat and shoes. Taking up his keys, he left through the front door, and gazed out into the night. It was cooler than on his previous excursion, and the fact that he remembered that proved to him that he must have done this then; it was no dream. He took a deep breath and walked across the street, heading to a rendezvous with something he suspected he'd already met several times in the past.

"Tonight, I'm going to remember everything that happens, that's all there is to it!"

. . .

The woods beckoned him, called to him. No fear, no anxiety, just an overwhelming sense of being brought back to... something. Those words resonated in his head again.

"Ona, cam, ona, cam..." He repeated them aloud, again like a mantra, hoping that they would clear his head and keep him focused. But as he entered the field, the waning moon lighting his way, a third word came to his mind.

"Ona, cam... Susan?"

He stopped.

"Wait, are they names? Ona? Cam? Susan? Who are they? Are they the ones showing up by my bed? Calling to me in the woods?"

He quickened his pace, being mindful not to trip.

"Last thing I need is to twist my ankle now, when I'm so close..."

The trees loomed before him, as they had the other night, but this time, he felt no sense of dread, only a burning desire for answers. One step after another, each bringing him closer to the revelation he craved. He thought he sensed a low hum from somewhere in the darkness of the forest, but he tried to ignore it and kept his pace. His right ear began to tingle, and then grow warm, and then burn. He grunted and rubbed it with his right hand, but he wouldn't be deterred.

His ear throbbing, he took his first steps into the woods. They were as dark and unforgiving as before, but this time, his keychain flashlight didn't work at all.

"Damn it! Even with a new battery."

Something was doing all of this, orchestrating it. He sighed and resigned himself to giving up control.

"Okay. I'm here. I'm doing what you want. If I have to play by your rules, so be it."

He was growing impatient, even annoyed. Setting aside the last of his doubts and apprehension, he strode forward, into the heart of the woods. After a short time, he saw a glow in the distance. He stopped for a moment and centered himself. He wanted to be sure that he was awake and in control of his own mind this time.

Resuming his stride, he saw the glow become brighter. In the distance, he could see a white luminance beyond a cluster of trees. It was large enough to be a machine of some kind, possibly a craft. It seemed to pulse, to grow brighter and dimmer, like some kind of beacon. He was reminded of the pulsing in his ear implant.

"Great, a UFO in the woods. A genuine, damned flying saucer."

He had a sense now of being watched, of things moving in the darkness just beyond his peripheral vision. They seemed to scurry about, and he could hear motion in the underbrush, even if he couldn't see them. He stopped again, trying to get a sense of what was out there, just beyond the edges of the light.

"I'm not here to play games," he announced. "I know that you've been barging into my life, probably for a long time. You put something in my ear the other night, didn't you? Show yourself. What do you want? I'm here, you brought me here. The least you can do is give me some answers now."

He heard a buzzing sound in his mind, but also in the air around him. He started to walk forward again, but wasn't quite sure if it was his choice, or if he was being compelled to do so. Something akin to whispering sounded through the buzz, and it seemed almost lighthearted, mischievous; there was a trace of laughter in it.

"So what are you? Aliens? Fairies? Are you exploring, or causing trouble? Are we all just a big joke to you?"

Something moved past him at a fast pace and drew his attention, but it was blurry when he tried to look at it. He squinted but couldn't focus. It was like it was both there and not there at the same time. He had a sense that the something was three entities of some kind, but they were gone before he could get any idea of what they were.

"That's not helpful!" he called out. "I can't exactly talk to you if you won't let me see you."

Your mind is adjusting, a calm, metallic voice sounded in his head. *Be patient and soon you will see beyond the veil.*

These words stopped him in his tracks. "Adjusting to what?"

We are out of time.

"What do you mean? Are you late? I came as soon as I sensed you. You can't leave now!"

We do not inhabit the same temporal reality as your body and mind. The device in your ear will help you adjust. Wait.

"Wait for what? I... oh!"

It was as if a fog lifted and the blurring around him stopped. It felt like putting on really good glasses, he noted with some amusement. In front of the glowing object, he saw the shadows of two figures, one short, and the other taller, though not as tall as a grown adult. Both were abnormally thin, at least as far as human physiques might go, but he was quite certain now that his hosts were something altogether very different.

He took a few more steps toward them to try to see them more clearly. They didn't move; it seemed that they wanted him to approach them.

"Who are you?" he asked out loud, grateful to hear the sound of his own voice; it gave him an anchor to reality in this mad circumstance.

It is more what we are, and what you are that is of concern. The voice was oddly mechanical and androgynous.

"I don't understand."

That is why you are here.

"We've done this before, haven't we? I mean, I've met you before, going back years, right? Going back to the owls in the window? I'm only remembering it now."

The taller figure seemed to incline its head forward a little. A nod of confirmation?

He risked another few steps, but nothing hindered his path now. He felt that he could walk right up to them if he wanted to… only, he wasn't sure that he wanted to, or if they did.

"What do you really want? Why is this happening to me?"

It is time for you to know, to learn, to understand.

"Okay… so what do I need to learn? To understand?"

You must come with us.

The shorter of the beings approached. It seemed to float over the ground with no effort. As it moved into the light, he could see its features clearly. It was light grey in color, very thin, with a large head. Its eyes were large, almond-shaped, and jet black. He saw no nose and only a small slit for a mouth.

"Damn it. Aliens!" he let out a long sigh.

To your time, yes, but we are not as we might seem. We are alike.

The taller of the two beings approached. Its head was in better proportion to its body, but it had similar facial features to its smaller companion, while its color seemed to be more of a light tan. Jace had the impression that it was female, but he didn't know why.

"How are we alike? How does that even make sense?"

The female stretched out a hand, its long spindly fingers beckoning him.

Come to us. Come with us. It is time to know. She projected at him.

"Come with you where?"

Out of time.

"Why do you keep saying that? Why…"

Jace felt as if he was being lifted up, but he saw nothing supporting him. He felt himself drawn toward the machine, the ship, whatever the glowing object was. He had the thought that this meeting was never going to be his choice. These things wanted him to join them, and he couldn't resist. The craft loomed before him now, its light bright but not blinding. He felt himself pass into it somehow, though he saw no doorway. Once again, he had the urge to close his eyes and sleep, like a drug had been injected into his system.

He struggled against it, but as he felt himself enter the craft, he gave in and knew no more.

CHAPTER 4

JACE OPENED HIS EYES WITH a start, as he'd done so many times in the past weeks. He expected to find himself in his bed, Sara sleeping next to him, heart beating over another nightmare. But all was dark, and he knew he was not in his bed; he was on a hard, even uncomfortable, surface. He tried to move his arms—or anything really—but found that he was unable to. He could turn his head, though, and he darted his glance from side to side, trying to get even the slightest idea of where he was. But the darkness was nearly total; only the faintest hint of some pale, amber light in the distance proved to him that he could see at all.

He should have panicked, he should have screamed. But an odd calm seemed to permeate his whole body. Somehow, he knew he wasn't in danger, that at the moment, this might be the safest place he could be. That didn't stop him from wanting to know what was happening though. He opened his mouth, which felt dry.

"Hello?" his voice was raspy and weak. "I'm here. Of course, you know that already, right? I came to you, I did what you wanted, I think. Why am I here, why can't I move? I'd like to move again, if that's okay."

He almost chuckled at his tone, bordering on sarcastic. "Hey, in a situation like this, what else can you do but laugh?" he said, a bit quieter.

The light in the distance seemed to grow. No, it was growing all around him, like a dimming light that was being turned up in stages. The blackness retreated, but at a very slow pace, and in the distance, there were still shadows. In those shadows, he could see forms. And now the fear began to take him. His heart raced and his breathing became more intense as he realized that since he couldn't move, he was completely at the mercy of whatever they might want to do to him. He forced himself to take a deep breath, trying very hard to remember the technique that Cassandra had taught him.

As if that's going to help right now! He rolled his eyes.

The forms moved toward him, again seeming to float above the ground in silence. As they emerged from the dark, he could see that they were the two he'd met in the forest... or were they? They looked the same, but maybe they always traveled in pairs, and this was a different duo. The shorter one was light grey, the taller one a pale tan color. Both had thin, spindly forms, and both had those beautiful but unnerving large, black, almond-shaped eyes. They seemed fearsome, yet oddly peaceful. He was at once repulsed and attracted to them, scared and comforted. His heart slowed and the fear washed away from him. They glided to his right side, and he was able to look at them directly now.

"Aliens," he sighed.

The taller of the two inclined her head and almost seemed to smile a bit with her tiny mouth.

In a sense, perhaps, her voice sounded in his head. It was cool, metallic, almost artificial, but somehow imbued with a genuine warmth and emotion.

"Why are you here?" he asked in his parched voice. "Why am *I* here?"

To learn. To know.

"Learn what? Know what? Is it me doing the learning and knowing, or you?"

The lights brightened around him, and with a quick glance around, he saw that he was in an oval-shaped chamber of some kind, with tiny points of light at the base of the curved wall, and a luminance coming from somewhere else that he couldn't see. It wasn't a "spaceship" in a classic sense: no white or metal walls, no flashing lights, no beeping. He had a strange sense that it was both machine and organic, as if it were alive, or partly so somehow, but that made no sense at all.

"Star Trek it is not," he joked to himself.

And yet, the woman's voice sounded in his head, *we share some of the aspirations and goals of that entertainment.*

"Wait," Jace said out loud, "you're telling me you've seen…"

His attention was diverted by a sound in the darkness and he thought he heard another being approaching. He could make out the shape of someone else, someone who looked decidedly more human, though this individual remained hidden in the shadows. Jace could only wonder at how many of them there were, and how many different kinds of aliens—if that's what they were—surrounded him.

"Is this an examination room?" he blurted out. "An operation room? 'Cause that's what you do, right? Take blood and other samples from people, collect them? Do stuff with them? That's what I've heard. Are we lab rats to you? Are you experimenting on us?"

He found that anger was swelling up in him again. How dare they bring him here? Subject him to this?

Our actions are for the greatest good of all. The taller one inclined her head again toward him.

"Easy for you to say, but from my point of view, you've kidnapped me and now I'm strapped to a table or something, and I can't move. That doesn't feel too 'good', if I'm being honest."

"It is for your own safety," the human-sounding voice of a man emerged from the dark. Was it the third being hidden in the shadows?

"So you can talk," he said, trying to focus on the being he thought he saw behind his two visitors.

Different orders use different means of communication, the female voice sounded in his head again.

"Orders? Orders of what? Are you different species? Are a bunch of you visiting Earth from other planets, like some federation thing?"

"It is more complex than that, but also, simpler," the human voice answered.

Jace sighed in frustration. "Look, can I move, please? It's pretty unnerving lying here while you're all watching me, and while you speak in riddles about who you are and what you're doing. I'd feel a lot better if I could at least have control over my own body."

It is for your protection, the woman's voice sounded.

"Protection from what?"

"You might call it a shift," the man's voice answered.

"A shift of what? To what? Come on, give me something here! Are we going to another planet?"

Another planet, yes. In some ways. Not the one you know, her voice answered.

"What the hell does that mean?"

In response, he felt a series of jolts that seemed to pass through the whole room, like turbulence on an airplane. He'd always hated that, so he was grateful to actually be immobile, at least in that moment. The two beings and the man in darkness were unaffected.

"What just happened?" Jace demanded, looking around at the room again.

"We've entered the stream," the concealed man answered.

"The stream? Like what, water? Are we in a river? Or an ocean? Is that where we're going?"

"The temporal stream," the man answered.

"Temporal? Like time?"

Another series of jolts shot a wave of panic through him. He'd never been fond of flying, and this just reminded him of why.

"Look, I'm not exactly thrilled to be here, okay? I came to you because you called out to me, and I remembered just enough to put things together so…"

Another jolt interrupted his words and he grimaced. Again, the three beings seemed completely unaffected.

"Can this machine, ship, whatever, please stop doing that?"

This is why you are bound, the woman's voice said in his mind.

Dizziness and slight nausea washed over Jace. "I don't feel great."

"It is an effect of the distortion," the man said. "It will pass."

Breathe as your mentor instructed, the woman's voice said. *Use that to bring yourself to your center.*

"What, you know about the hypnosis?" Jace demanded.

It is how we prepared you to be ready. Ms. Hill has helped us in the past.

"Wait, you did that? Like you nudged me to go get hypnotized? She knows about you?"

You were almost ready, but still needed to unlock some things in your mind that were hidden. Things you did not want to see.

A fourth jolt rocked the room.

"Like owls looking in my bedroom window at night?"

"A mask memory, to help your mind cope with the experience," the man, still hiding in the dark, answered. "I have found that our brains do not function on the same level as theirs, and so we construct mental images to protect ourselves and make sense of what we are seeing."

"Who are you, damn it? Who are they?" He addressed his anger to the man in the shadows.

A fifth jolt shot through the chamber, though this time, it was far less severe. Again his visitors seemed unaffected, as if they'd done this many times.

We will arrive soon, the woman projected, turning her head slightly to her left, as if looking at something beyond his field of vision.

"Where?" Jace again demanded.

"The better word," the man in darkness said, "is: when?"

• • •

I must have blacked out, he thought. Jace opened his eyes—again—and looked around. He seemed to be in a different room, but one that was still lit in the same manner as where he'd been held before. He was relieved to find that he could move his hands and arms. A quick test of his legs and feet proved that they were under his control, too. He sat up a little, supporting himself with his elbows on the table where he was lying. He looked around, but saw nothing distinct, just the murky shadows of a room that seemed to have none of the things one would expect in an alien ship.

"Or a time machine," he mused. "What the hell does that even mean? Who are these people?"

"We're more alike than you might imagine."

It was the voice of the man in the shadows, and Jace could just make out his shape in the dark at the opposite end of the room.

"You seem to enjoy hanging out in the dark, Jace quipped. "Care to step into the light and tell me who you are?"

He saw the figure begin to move. In a moment a man stood before him. It was definitely a man, not one of those other beings. Jace was both relieved and disappointed. He was of normal height, with shoulder-length hair that was silvery, rather than grey, but his face looked younger. There was something else about him… was it the eyes? Something that seemed a bit different.

"I feel like I know you, or should," Jace said, words that surprised him. Why would he know this mystery man?

"It's very possible," the man replied. "We have met before."

"We have? Where?"

"At your place of work. I was stationed in a different department, but there was a social event where we talked briefly, last spring."

"Hm. All right, if you say so. Yeah, yeah, now that I think about it, I do remember you. We said something about, I don't know, some engineering thing? I remember thinking you looked a little weird. Oh, sorry."

"No apologies necessary. My appearance is somewhat different from yours, or other humans of your time."

"Okay, what the hell does that even mean?" Jace was getting annoyed again. "Seriously, can somebody *please* tell me what's going on?"

"It's all rather complicated, I'm afraid."

"I'm an engineer; I'll figure it out!"

"I have no doubt. And that's why we've watched you."

"Watched me? You mean like, through my window? Coming into my bedroom at night? That kind of watching?" Jace had the momentary thought of standing up and threatening to punch the man, but for some reason, the feeling passed almost as soon as it came over him.

"That and more."

"Why? Tell me!"

"You are important."

"Well, thanks; that explains everything."

"You and others like you are vital to our mission."

"And that mission would be what, exactly?"

"Protecting and preserving the world, allowing it to renew itself."

"Wait, are you guys like some kind of hippy cult, or eco-terrorists, or something? Are you messing with me? I promise I don't have access to any secrets. Just let me go, and we can forget all about it."

"I assure you, terrorism as you define it is the farthest thing possible from our goal. You do not recall seeing me at any other time?"

Jace shook his head. "Should I? I mean we can play twenty questions here, or you can just tell me."

"At your place of learning, what you called high school. I was there, as well. I posed as an office worker. I was rather surprised that you didn't recognize me when we met at your place of employment, but I took the risk."

"I'm not really good with faces, I guess."

"Perhaps it was better for me, then," the man shrugged a little.

"So, what," Jace demanded, "you've been watching me for twenty years? Like, stalking me?"

"No, no stalking. And only for a very short time."

"But you just said you worked at my high school, so you've obviously been around for a while; looking pretty good for your age, by the way."

The man smiled a little. "No, I observed you there, and then again in another time, I observed you at your work place. Two different times, but only a short journey for me."

"Oh, right," Jace said with sarcasm, "because you're time travelers. So… you just popped in for a few weeks to spy on me in high school, jumped in your time machine, and decided to come work at my company when I was all grown up."

"That's a simplified way of stating it, but essentially, it's correct, yes. There were other occasions in between, as well."

"Of course there were."

"You were one of several young people identified as being of use to our mission, and it was my task to get a closer look at you, without being too suspicious."

"Sure, because a guy with silvery hair and unusual eyes checking out high school teenagers isn't suspicious at all."

"We were discreet."

"No doubt. So what… that owl I remembered? In my window? That was you?"

"That was one of the transformed. They needed to get a closer look at you."

"The transformed?"

"The ones who were near you earlier as we traveled. Those we visit often liken them to owls or other animals, so it is a simple matter to implant a mask memory over what they really see. An owl is quite effective for that. If our visitation is remembered at all, which we take pains to prevent, the person in question will usually only remember an animal."

"You said, 'as we traveled,'" Jace almost interrupted. "Where are we now?"

"On Earth."

"Fine, but where?"

"Near what you know as North Carolina, the western portion of it."

"So we flew down here in your spaceship?"

"Something like that, only it's not meant for space travel."

"Look," Jace sighed, "I'm getting tired of this. Can you please just tell me where I am exactly, and why I'm, here? Because seriously, right now, I'm already thinking about the massive report I'm going to be filing with the police if you don't tell me exactly what's going on, and why you've basically kidnapped me!"

"You came to us of your own accord."

"Because you wouldn't leave me alone! Because you're in my head, doing things. You're putting… stuff in my ear that burns and then hounding me until I do what you want."

"The implant was necessary to bring you here. It allowed your body to adjust to the stresses of temporal dislocation more easily. You might still have felt a bit sick, and if so, I apologize."

"Yeah, I did, so be glad I didn't puke all over your… whatever this place is… ship? Gigantic insect? Who knows? Now, one more time: what's going on, and where the hell am I?"

"At this moment, you are approximately 1,000 years in the future, and everything you ever knew is gone."

• • •

Jace reeled at these words. *This is nuts, this is insane.* Lightheadedness threatened to overwhelm him for a moment, but he shook his head to fight it off. He looked up again at his visitor. The man seemed impassive, even emotionless, but there was something sincere about him. Even if this story was nonsense, Jace had the feeling that he at least believed what he was saying.

"All right," Jace stammered. "Okay fine. We're in 'the future.' Why? What's so special about this place that you have to rip me out of my own time and bring me here?"

"Because this is where the restoration of the Earth is happening. This is where healing, reconciliation, and renewal will be brought to this ancient and weary planet, so that she might live and thrive again."

"So you *are* like, environmentalists, then?"

"Far more than that. We are bio-engineers. We are re-seeders. We seek to restore balance."

"What happened? In those centuries, I mean?"

"You see the way that world is now in your time, teetering on the brink of disaster. Every day, you read new reports of environmental damage, severe fluctuations in climate. While many are concerned about this, those in power ignore the warning signs, or are paid to ignore them. Everyone is worried, but everyone also seems to think it will never happen, or that your science will somehow miraculously solve the problems facing you. And so, the human race goes about its business, and tries not to think about the looming disaster in front of it."

"But a disaster happens?'

"Several of them, over a succession of many years. The Gulf Stream in the Atlantic fluctuates and shuts down, storms become far more severe, dry areas become drier, wet areas are hit with more rain than they ever thought possible. As the weather and climate move into radically unpredictable currents, millions of people are displaced and must flee their homes. Whole nations are upended. Droughts and famines are common place. Millions starve, while wealthy nations try to hoard what they have and keep out those fleeing from the disasters.

"This will be the lot of the human race for much of the twenty-first century, beginning about the year 2030. By the century's end, there will be vast inequality and inequity among nations. Extreme heat and extreme cold will cause many to seek refuge underground. Dictators and despots will arise, more so than even in your own time, and will threaten war if their demands are not met. Acts of terrorism will increase. Harsh words will be shouted at international meetings. By the beginning of the twenty-second century, the world will be a proverbial powder keg, ready to explode, and explode it shall.

"In 2108, an assassination of a major political figure will set off a chain of events, not unlike that which begat the First World War. It will spiral out of control as nations line up to take sides. There will be ground conflicts, and ultimately, a limited nuclear exchange."

Jace's eyes widened. "What?"

"Thankfully, not enough to obliterate life on Earth, but the damage will be done in certain areas, and leave those regions irradiated and unliveable. Some other areas will be relatively untouched, but as radiation and other pollutants drift around the world, all will be touched by them. Human fertility will decline, as will that of many animal species. Those closest to the blast areas will be poisoned and even suffer mutations. The human population will go into a sharp decline by 2250, as pollution, disease, poor weather, and starvation all take their toll. More and more people will retreat underground."

Jace stared at the floor and shook his head.

"Those remaining scientists will attempt to address the problems, but their solutions will only make matters worse. Using nanotechnologies and other inventions, they will attempt to clean the ground and sky, but their creations will backfire, as these tiny replicating robots take on a life of their own. In order to prevent them from devouring all remaining life, a team of researchers introduce a kind of mechanical plague, a synthetic bio-mechanical virus to destroy the nanobots, or at least render them inert. And in this, they are successful, but the virus somehow is able to jump species and infect humans. It does not kill them, but it accelerates the mutated genes already in their bodies from a generation of radioactivity, and it begins to… change them. "

"Change them?"

"Infants are born smaller, looking more and more emaciated in their bodies, while their heads grow to a normal size. Because of the dimmer sunlight thanks to pollution, climate change, and living in underground, their eyes begin to grow larger with each generation, trying to take in more of the light. Over several hundred years, an evolutionary process that might have taken a half a million years or more takes place in the humans remaining. They begin to resemble those beings that your gaudy newspapers call aliens."

Jace rubbed his hands on his face. "This is just, I can't, what?"

"The next several centuries are a bleak age for these rapidly transforming humans," his visitor continued. "It seems as if the human species might go extinct. But even in this dark age, there is light, there is hope. They find that with their evolution comes an expanded understanding of the world, of science, and even the flow of time. They are able to unlock the secrets of traveling through the time stream, at first only in short bursts and very recently, but as their understanding increases, they are able to slip farther and farther back through time. Initially, they only want to observe, to understand what went so horribly wrong. But as they learn more and more, they come to realize that they can interact with those in their past, and for some, this gives them an idea."

"An idea about what?" Jace looked up from his hands, struggling to take all of this in.

"The world of this time has degraded, through a combination of pollution and radiation. Many species have gone extinct, and biodiversity is severely damaged. But what if it were possible to restart that process? What if, by harvesting samples of hundreds of thousands of animals and plants from the past and bringing them forward into this time, these new humans—future humans to you—could re-seed and regrow the world? Despite the damage done from radiation, all is not lost. They have discovered species of fungi—mushrooms—that absorb radioactive materials with no trace left in the environment. Would it be possible to rebuild and repopulate the Earth? To bring back the grandeur of its life? Its biodiversity? Fortunately, the answer is yes."

"So, you're trying to save your world by coming back to the past and doing what? Gathering seeds and mushrooms? Okay fine, but what about us? Humans?"

"We are taking seed from all things."

"Wait, hold on, you mean…"

"The humans you saw earlier, the ones you have called aliens, are superior to you in mental capacities. They have lost the ability to speak, but can project their thoughts into your head. They are remarkable beings, a masterpiece of evolution, even if it was forced on them much sooner than should have been the case. But what they have great difficulty in doing is reproducing. Many have even taken to artificially enhancing their forms with mechanical additions to live longer. This is why some humans who are, as you say, 'abducted,' have said that the greys seem more like robots than living beings. In one sense, that's true."

Jace shook his head and looked back to the floor.

"But there is enough genetic material within them, no matter how degraded, that they can cross it with healthy humans from the past and create a new species of human, one that will be robust, can reproduce, and will have the advanced mental capacities that the greys possess. They are seeking to create a hybrid species between what they are and what you are, one that will thrive in the new world they are building, one where new humans can have a second chance."

"But how would these humans… I mean, wouldn't they look really weird?"

"'Weird' is in the eye of the beholder, to quote a phrase from your time. And with each generation of hybridization, the new beings take on more of the appearance of humans from before. I am one such example. You can think of me as a 'seven-eighths hybrid,' if you like. My appearance is not exactly that of a previous human, but it is close enough that I can move about in your world while drawing very little attention. My hair and my eyes are the only things that mark me as different."

"So, human sperm and ova are taken from people in my time…"

"And earlier times."

"And hybridized with genetic material from yours to make new humans?"

"Essentially."

"Okay, but these people, the ones you collect… samples from. Do they agree to this? It doesn't seem very ethical to go around doing that without permission." Jace could hardly believe he was even having this conversation.

"At first, the mission seemed too urgent to worry overly much about that, but yes, you're right. We can hardly claim to be doing something for a noble purpose, if we take what is not ours without that permission. And so, we have sought the consent of those we visit, and in most cases, we obtain it."

"And for those that say no?"

"We release them, of course. With no memories to burden them."

"Okay, but how do you choose? Who gets picked?"

"It is a combination of both genetic qualities and personality traits. Beings such as I observe humans from earlier times all over the world, in differing times. There are qualities we look for, but no one is excluded from consideration. All of humanity has richness to offer."

"Okay, okay, but, why am I here? I'm not…" his heart raced. "I'm not one of these hybrids am I?"

"No"

Jace was relieved, even if he wasn't sure why.

"But your genetic material was deemed acceptable long ago, when I first monitored you in your school."

These words hit Jace like a sledge hammer.

"What?"

"We approached you later when you were in your college and offered a chance to contribute to our gene pool. You readily agreed."

"Hang on, I did *not* do that!"

"You did, but you are struggling to remember. The incident with seeing the owl? It happened both in your teenage years and beyond. The doctor you work with in your own time would have unlocked that memory soon, but it seems better to tell you about it now, and let those memories come back to you as they will. You willingly donated your reproductive material to us in aid of our goal."

Jace felt dizzy, like he was about to black out. He put his head down in his hands again, certain now that he was going mad. None of this was happening; it wasn't even possible. He could hear the pounding of his heart in his ears. It was so strong that he barely heard or understood the hybrid's next words:

"Would you like to meet your other family?"

CHAPTER 5

"NO, NO, NO!"

Jace was vaguely aware of hearing his own voice and stumbling forward, somewhere. He couldn't focus, couldn't think. Everything around him was a blur.

"This is wrong, this is crazy!"

He felt sick to his stomach again, and barely kept himself from falling to his knees and retching. All he could do was try to escape, try to find a way out.

"Gotta get out of here. This is a trick, this is…"

He managed to spot something in front of him, a small, grey-colored being, but instead of crashing into it, it seemed to blur out of existence for a half-second and reappear to his left.

He had enough focus now to see that he was in a long hallway, dimly lit and curving to the right. But he had no idea how he'd come to be there, or where "there" even was. He reached out to touch a wall and steady himself. It felt odd: warm one moment, cool the next. It seemed to be oscillating, almost as if it were…

"Breathing?"

He shook off his confusion and pressed on, mindful only of his own safety, his own sanity, and a panicked urge to get out of this awful place.

"Don't know what they did, why…"

Jace.

The woman's voice sounded inside his head. "Get out of my mind! Get out!" Jace snarled, looking around for any sign of her… it… whatever it was.

Please, let us help you.

"You've already done enough! Let me out of this place… now!"

That is not possible, I'm afraid.

"The hell it isn't! You put me in here; you take me back… now!"

A wave of nausea washed over him, and he doubled over, though thankfully, he didn't expel the contents of his stomach. He looked up again, hot and sweating, certain that someone was behind him.

"Gotta be a way out of here… there has to be!"

But in front of him, there was nothing but the long hall, stretching away in an endless curve. No doors, no side halls, just that endless curve, endless…

"Damn it! Am I running in a circle?" he gasped as he stopped to catch his breath.

Jace.

"Enough! Enough of this! Who the hell are you really? What did you do to me? Where am I?"

If you will just let us explain further…

"No! No more of your BS about time travel, genetic breeding, the future, whatever. I want the truth! Now!"

"We can give you that," the seven-eighths hybrid's voice came from somewhere in front of him. "But you will have to trust us."

"Why should I?" Jace blurted out between heavy gasps of humid air.

"You said that you wanted the truth." The hybrid appeared from the shadows in front of him. "And we have given you that. But I understand that you require further proof." He reached out one hand. "If you will come with me."

"And do what? Meet my 'family'? Do you know how ridiculous that sounds?"

"I do. And no, we will not take you to meet them. Not yet. I can see now that you need further convincing. It was a mistake for us to assume that you had recovered enough of your memories to trust us fully. I apologize. But I will show you something, if you'll come with me."

Jace drew himself up, feeling better, more composed. "You gave me something, didn't you? Back in the forest. That's what this is. You drugged me, took me to some warehouse, you're playing up this BS time travel sci-fi crap because you want something. Who are you? A rival company? Is this corporate espionage? Look, I told you: I don't know any juicy secrets; that's way above my pay grade. I'm just an engineer. If you want that kind of stuff, you'll have to find someone else."

"We do not need your company's technological secrets, I can assure you." The hybrid looked almost amused. "Though it might be entertaining to see what they have come up with."

"I'm glad you find this all funny," Jace snapped.

The hybrid's face softened. "We are on your side, Jace, I promise you. You want proof that we are who we say we are and that you are where we say you are. I understand that. If you will come with me, I can show you."

"Why should I trust you? How do I know that you're not gonna just take me somewhere and shoot me, now that I've told you I don't know anything valuable?"

"You don't, but there is no way that I can prove that, either. So, we are at an impasse. We can stand here for a long time talking at one another, or you can come with me. The choice is yours, of course."

"I want to leave, I want to go home."

"And you will. We shall return you right to the moment that you left. But first, we must show you things and speak with you further."

"Why?"

"We need your help, Jace. Yours and that of thousands of other humans from the past. Our project is vast and ongoing." He held out his hand again. "Please… come with me? I will show you the proof that you need."

Jace looked down and sighed. He shook his head and chuckled. "This is all ridiculous. All of it. None of it's real, you're all just having me on." He looked up. "Okay, all right, fine, you win. I'll go with you. Show me this amazing thing you want to show me, convince me that you're the real deal, and maybe I'll stay around for a bit. But if you're lying, or trying to screw me over, I swear you'll be sorry!"

The hybrid nodded. "That seems a fair bargain. Come along"

. . .

Jace let himself be led through a series of corridors that he never would have noticed in his distressed state. Occasionally, he passed one of the greys who moved silently and didn't acknowledge him. When Jace strained get a better look at one of their faces, they seemed to be able to blur out his perception and make it hard for him to focus.

"Many of them don't like being looked at by outsiders," the hybrid said. "Even after centuries of mutations and change, some are still very self-conscious."

"What are they? I mean really?"

"They are human, like you and I, only different. As I said, mutations from radiation and the 'cure' for it caused them to change appearance rapidly from one generation to the next. The heat that plagued many parts of the Earth made dwelling on the surface unbearable, and so they sought refuge underground. The natural tendency for the eyes of species to grow larger in darker environments was accelerated a thousand-fold, thus giving them the appearance you see now... or don't see." He smirked.

"What about the other one. The... woman?" Jace felt odd calling the taller being that, but that was what she seemed to be.

"The mutations took different forms in different parts of the world, so not every group of humans changed in the same ways. There are others that you haven't seen yet. Some are old, very old, and as I've said, they keep themselves alive with mechanical enhancements, cybernetics, if you will. That is why some seem to be almost robotic in their movements, more machine than living. In a sense that's what they are. "

"And you said they can't reproduce?"

"Most cannot. Not anymore, which is why they have initiated this genetic breeding program. Their brains are magnificent, a pinnacle of evolution, but their bodies are weak and decaying, and without the input of fresh genetic material, the human species would become extinct in another century or two, anyway. But we have a chance to save ourselves. And not only that, to bring back the countless species that were harmed or lost in the past thousand years and longer. We can cleanse the world of its toxins, reintroduce the flora and fauna, and rebuild a better humanity. Gaia is very sick, but we can still renew her, with the help of people like you."

They had reached a portal at a dead end in the corridor. The hybrid turned to Jace. "Now you will see."

With a wave of his hand, the portal opened and they stepped into what looked like an elevator.

"So you still use these in the thirty-first century?" Jace quipped. "Can't we just 'beam up' to wherever we're going?"

"Teleportation has some limits," the hybrid said without a trace of irony or joking.

"But… you can do it?"

"Of course, it's essential to some of our missions. But it must be done with care. The transfer of matter into energy and its reassembly is a complex process, and even with our knowledge, things sometimes go wrong. It's not as easy as it looks in movies and television."

Jace had the sense of rising, though he heard no mechanical sounds and saw nothing indicating that they were moving at all. Sometime later the sensation stopped.

"We are here," the hybrid said with a smile.

"Where's 'here'?"

The hybrid looked at him with calm assurance. "It's time for you to see our world."

• • •

Jace squinted in the late afternoon light. By the position of the sun, he knew he was looking west. The sunset was orange, but with hints of other colors: red, purple, even a bit of blue. It was unlike any sunset he'd ever seen. As his eyes adjusted, he took a deep breath. The air was clean and clear, but somehow smelled different. Again, it was unlike any scent he'd encountered.

"Subtle atmospheric differences still linger, after a thousand years of change and upheaval," the hybrid said. "It's why the sunlight looks a bit different and the air smells unusual to you. It's partially those changes, and also the work that we've done to reclaim it."

Jace focused on the landscape. They were surrounded by rolling hills, some of which had trees that looked familiar; a whole forest spread into the distance on his left. But to his right…

"Wait, what are those?" he pointed as his eyes widened.

The hybrid smiled. "Ah yes, the *megagaricus*. Quite unusual if you've never seen them."

Jace's mouth dropped open as he beheld vast mushrooms, the size of small trees, looming over him, like some bizarre scene from *Alice in Wonderland*. A whole forest of white mushrooms and some other types stood before him.

H-how?" he started.

"Giant fungi once were found across the Earth in prehistoric times. We were able to work with surviving species to create these impressive hybrids and bring them back to their full glory. You see, even with the radiation and climate disasters, many fungi underground were not affected. They can thrive regardless of conditions up above, in vast colonies that are miles wide. Most people in your time are barely even aware of their existence, but their potential for everything from food to medicine to pollution control is almost unlimited. Without them, we wouldn't be able to do what we're doing. Portions of living colonies have been grafted into our technology, our 'ships,' if you will, which allows for quicker interfacing and use."

"Wait," Jace stared at him, "you're saying that we were traveling inside a gigantic mushroom?!"

The hybrid chuckled. "That's a bit of an oversimplification. It's rather that their networks allow us to make use of the technology that we have in a more efficient way, an effective melding of the living and the machine. Some of the greys have even been able to use fungi structures to help preserve their bodies. It's known among abductees that the greys can sometimes have a faint mushroom smell. That's why."

Jace looked back. "They're, they're, incredible! And you eat them?"

"They have many purposes, but harvesting for food is certainly one of them."

"Wow, I hope you have a lot of garlic and olive oil to go with them!" Jace found himself chuckling, despite the sheer craziness of this whole situation.

"Do you believe me now?" The hybrid turned to look at him.

"I mean…" Jace looked around again, back at the elevator. It opened from the side of a hill, with nothing else unusual about it, just shrubs, along with grass and normal-looking trees. "This might still just be a hallucination, right? You could've doped me up with something and this is all happening in my mind."

"I suppose anything's possible, but to what end? If we were a corporate espionage team from your own time, what would be the point in creating," he gestured with one had, "this?"

Jace sighed. "Fair enough. Okay, so I'm actually in the freaking thirty-first century, and we're in Appalachia?"

"We are indeed. It was one of the areas less affected by the traumas of the twenty-first and twenty-second centuries, so it seemed prudent to begin our work here, and in other select locations around the world, where we could see results quickly. I'd offer to take you for a walk, but there isn't that much to see, beyond forest and mushrooms. Our compound is all underground."

"Why is that?"

"Because that was where it was constructed when the environmental conditions were not good, centuries ago. We've come a long way since with improvements to the biosphere, and we would like to begin constructing settlements above ground, but for now, it seems prudent to let the Earth continue to heal without too much of our interference."

Jace sighed. "This is… this is a lot."

"I understand."

"Do you? Do you really? Do you have any idea what it's like to find out that your life is a, well maybe not a lie, but something totally different than what you thought it was?"

"Honestly, I do not, but I am sympathetic. I have seen this many times over the years, the struggle I mean. When someone realizes that there is so much more to their reality than they thought. It is not our intention to shock or upset, I promise you. We do this because there is a great need."

"So why am I here? What is it you really want me to do? You already have my… DNA, don't you? Can't you just create more people from it? Because if you can't, I'm sorry but I'm not letting you do that again!"

The hybrid shook his head. "That's not why you were awakened. Not why you were brought here."

"So what is it, then? Do you want me to help pick giant mushrooms?"

To Jace's surprise, the hybrid burst out laughing. "Would that it were something as simple as that. No, no it's a bit more involved, I confess."

"Okay, okay," Jace pressed, but really not seeing the humor in his situation. "So? What?"

"Come," the hybrid motioned. "It will be getting dark soon, and we can talk more back in the compound."

• • •

Jace followed his mysterious captor/host back into the elevator, down the shaft and into another area of what seemed to be a vast structure. He was led through rooms with familiar and unfamiliar technology, and he saw a variety of beings, from those that were almost human to a handful that looked like the greys. There were some like the woman who spoke to him in his mind, and a few others that were unlike anything he'd seen before, including a few who were even shorter, had dark grey skin and small, black eyes. They all seemed to be going about their tasks with diligence, not speaking to one another, not showing any signs of camaraderie, friendship, or even acknowledging each other's existence.

"Are all of these... people, really human?" he whispered as they passed out of one particularly crowded work area.

"In varying degrees, yes."

They entered into another long hall.

"Okay, so what about actual aliens? Like, that's what we've always figured you all are, I mean, those that believe in aliens. But are there, you know, 'real' aliens out there?"

"Oh yes, quite a few." The hybrid walked on, saying nothing else.

"Wait, that's it? That's all you're gonna say. Come on, man! I've just asked you one of the most important questions humanity has, you know, the whole 'are we alone in the universe?' thing, and you just tell me aliens are real and then clam up?"

The hybrid looked back at him, a hint of annoyance on his face. "We can talk more about it later. But for now, we need to focus on why you are here, and what we want from you."

Jace thought about arguing the point, but decided to let it go. He realized that he wasn't in any position to make demands. Whether he was a guest or a prisoner, these beings held all the cards for the moment. He let out another sigh and followed the hybrid down a side corridor, spotting what looked like a glowing chamber in the distance.

"You never told me your name," Jace tried changing the subject and making lighter conversation.

"Questions later," the hybrid commanded. "For now, you must listen to what we have to tell you. It is imperative that you fully understand why you are here, and what is expected of you."

"Expected of me?" Jace grew angry again. "As far as I'm concerned, I don't owe any of you anything!"

The hybrid turned to look at him. "It was part of the agreement you made with us, when we approached you as a younger man."

"Well, I don't remember agreeing to anything."

"You will in time. Please step in."

Jace entered a circular chamber with what looked like a round table in the middle. Standing about it was the tan-colored female being he'd now seen several times. She was wearing what looked like a thin white gown. Next to her was the same shorter grey (at least he assumed it was the same one). A trio of other greys stood nearby, but Jace had a difficult time focusing on them. Once again, every time he tried to look directly at them, they seemed to fade out or blur, and he could only see them from his peripheral vision. Standing behind them was another woman, one who looked fully human, save for her platinum-colored hair and striking blue-grey eyes. She was tall, towering over the others, and Jace thought that she might be Scandinavian.

Welcome, Jace, a familiar voice—hers—sounded in his head. He thought he saw her incline her head slightly.

"We trust you are adapting and settling in," the Nordic woman said, in a voice that was quieter and softer than he might have imagined it would be. Her accent definitely suggested that she was from a Nordic country.

"Um… not really," he said, realizing that he sounded more off-putting and rude than he intended. "I mean no disrespect, but this is all way too much to take in. I hope you can all appreciate that."

"Of course," the Nordic woman answered.

The mysterious tan being again inclined her head, as if understanding his concerns. He continued to feel drawn to her and comforted by her presence, though he didn't understand why.

"Please," the Nordic woman gestured with one hand. "Come and join us. We wish to tell you many things and explain fully why you are here."

"That's great," Jace said with a sigh, "because right now, I'm really struggling with all of this and I just want to know what's going on."

"I understand," she answered. "All will be made clear presently. But suffice to say that you are a perfect candidate."

"Candidate? For what?"

"To undertake a mission on our behalf throughout time."

. . .

"Woah, woah, wait a minute. Just wait a damned minute! What the hell are you talking about?!" Jace stopped in his tracks and stared back at each of them in turn, anger welling up inside of him again. "A mission? Who do you think I am? James Bond? Come on, stop jerking me around... why am I *really* here?"

"In order to complete our tasks," the hybrid said, "we have to journey back to various points in time, mostly from the twenty-first century and earlier."

"So you've told me," Jace countered, "several times."

"But not every mission is about collecting samples of DNA and other genetic material," the hybrid continued. "There are some that require a more hands-on approach, a task that, as you can see by looking at us, we are not well suited for."

"What do you mean, 'hands on'?" Jace's eyes narrowed.

"By traveling through time, we invite certain... risks," the Nordic woman said. "While we can mostly operate undetected, if people see us, or learn about us, we must wipe their memories. Too much knowledge about us could have devastating effects on the time line."

"We're not trying to change history," the hybrid added, "only trying to take what we need from it and stay out of its way."

Jace looked down and shook his head again. "Hold on," he looked up. "If your actions can change history, then why not just go back in time to the point where humanity really started screwing up the climate, or back to when we came up with nuclear weapons? Why not just alter those things and prevent any of what… happened here from happening to begin with? Save yourselves some trouble."

"Because the outcome would be completely unknown," the Nordic woman answered. If we made such a major change, we might invite an even greater catastrophe instead. We cannot take the risk. We must preserve what has already happened and seek to repair what we can."

"Sorry, but you… don't seem like the others." Jace eyed her with more attention.

"I'm not. I am fully human, and like you, I am from the past."

"So you work for them, then?" Jace motioned to the others. "You go on covert missions to do the things they can't?"

"That is a good enough summary," she said with a nod.

"So, where are you from? *When* are you from?" Jace could barely believe he was even asking these questions.

"I was born in the ninth century, in what is now Norway."

"And you hooked up with these folks… how?"

She smiled. "That is a long story. Perhaps I can tell you on the mission."

Jace blew out a puff of air. "I can't even believe I'm saying this. Okay, what kind of mission? What are we talking about?"

"Occasionally, some of our work in the past does cause… minor upsets to the timeline, but if these are left unrepaired, they might potentially lead to greater problems," the hybrid explained.

"Ah, so you want me to go around cleaning up your messes?" Jace quipped.

"Again, it's a bit more complex than that," the hybrid answered without a trace of emotion, neither humor nor defense.

"Okay, so," Jace threw up his hands, "what is it? What do you want me to do?"

"We would like to have you help with a… small problem in the past," the Nordic woman said.

"How small?" Jace's clenched his jaw.

"We need you to prevent a murder," the hybrid answered.

"Oh, is that all?" Jace threw up his hands again. "Sure! No problem! What, am I going to be a body guard? Throw myself in front of someone and take a bullet for them? Who is it? I should know. Is it somebody famous, at least?"

"Not exactly. Well, it is someone well known in certain circles, though of no consequence to most of the people living in your time."

"So not a movie star, then? Okay, what? A politician? A CEO? Some other bigwig that can't take care of themselves?"

The hybrid smiled slightly. "We want you to help save the life of a king in early fourteenth-century England."

Jace guffawed in spite of himself. "You… you're joking, right? Right? Come on, I can accept the future and the giant mushrooms, and the humans with bug eyes, but come the hell on… a king in the fourteenth century? What's so important about him? I mean, weren't they all stabbing each other in the backs then, anyway? What difference does it make?"

"It's actually not about him," the hybrid answered. "It's about the importance of his son, and then his son's descendants, one of whom will be a key twenty-second century scientist who discovers some of the methods that will help eventually rebuild civilization in the aftermath of the Torments."

"The Torments?"

"Sorry, what we sometimes call the centuries after the collapse of civilization," the hybrid explained. "Dr. Sonja Porter. Without this woman's work in an underground bunker, and those who built on it in later decades and centuries, we would not have the blueprint needed to repair the world. If this medieval king dies, his son—also a king—will never be born, and so she will never be born centuries later. And without her, everything we have tried to do will be lost."

"But, if you messed something up back then," Jace countered "wouldn't this assassination have already happened? Wouldn't you have noticed something by now?"

"Yes, it did," the hybrid answered. "And we're already seeing signs of it. A portion of our complex here, along with all those living and working in it, simply vanished. Erased from time. More disruptions will follow as the ripples of what happened in those dark days take full effect. Which is why we cannot wait much longer."

Jace sighed. "And you want to trust me—a complete novice—to do this, because why?"

"Because you are fully human and will pass for those you must interact with," the hybrid said. "And you agreed long ago to assist us when we might need you."

"And again, I have no memory of that at all. You're asking me to take a lot on trust."

"You do not have to agree, yet," the Nordic woman replied. "But we would like you to think it over. Please. And soon."

Jace looked at her again. "Would you be going with me?"

"Yes, of course."

"And… you'll tell me exactly what I need to do."

"To the smallest detail," the hybrid said.

"I can't even believe I'm saying this, but okay, if I agree to help you, will I get to go back to my own time?"

"Of course," the hybrid answered. "You will not be held against your will here, I promise. In fact, you can go there first to prepare, if you'd like, to the very moment that you left. And see your wife and children before we depart."

"Because I might not be coming back?"

"There is always a risk associated with these ventures."

"You're not really selling this too well, you know," Jace half-joked. "Fine, okay, okay, I get it. I have a chance to do something amazing, something that pretty much no one gets to do. And as an engineer with an interest in science, that's pretty cool. Freaking time travel!" He turned to the Nordic woman. "But if we're going to work together, I need to know your name, at least."

"In my own time, I was called Tora."

"And now?"

"Tora is good," she said with a slight smile.

"I can go with that," Jace said. He turned to the hybrid. "And how about you? Can I at least know what to call you?"

"My name is Aereon."

"Nice to meet you," Jace said with a hint of sarcasm. He looked at the others, so alien in appearance. "What may I call all of you?"

We do not use such designations, the mysterious woman answered in his mind. *We take part in a knowing and connection at a deep level that is more personal and intimate than a mere name can offer. But if you wish, you may call me Lyffe.*

"Life?" Jace asked.

She nodded her head slightly. *Close enough.*

"So, what do I have to do?" Jace looked around at all of them.

"Come with me," Aereon said, "and we can prepare you. Oh, and the offer still stands, if you wish to meet the family you have helped to create in this time."

Jace sighed. "I suppose I should. This is going to be surreal. All right then, take me to them."

CHAPTER 6

"THE WORLD OF THE PAST will be unlike anything you've ever known," Aereon explained as they walked to what Jace assumed was a training room. "You must be extremely careful in how you interact with everyone. The whole point is to be as inconspicuous as possible. We want to leave very little evidence we were there, whether physical or emotional."

"You said we're going back to England in the early fourteenth century," Jace said.

"Correct."

"Okay fine, but how am I going to understand what anyone says? I vaguely remember English literature in high school covering Chaucer and stuff, and it made no sense to me, especially when the teacher read it out loud as it would have sounded. And this time is like seventy years at least before that, right?"

"No need to worry on that front," Aereon said with a slight smile, while still looking straight ahead. "We have crafted a device that allows you to hear anything spoken to you in twenty-first century English, and for your words to sound like fourteenth-century English to them. It's small and you can wear it hidden on your clothing."

Jace came to a halt. "Wait, like a universal translator?"

Aereon stopped and nodded, looking at him. "Similar to those in the science fiction dramas of your own time. Humans have been actively inventing new wonders over the last several centuries, you see. You'll be surprised by what we've come up with."

"I'm not sure anything will surprise me anymore," Jace sighed, resuming his pace again.

"We'll see," was all that Aereon would say.

They took a side passage and came to another circular room. Jace noted that all the rooms in this complex looked oddly similar, but seemed to change as their function was revealed: dimly lit, with tan colored walls, while chairs, tables, and other furnishings seemed to be stored under the floor or in the walls until they were needed. But this room remained empty even after they arrived. Empty except for Tora, who stood in the middle, holding a device in her hands that Jace didn't recognize. She attached it to her forearm, rather like a wrist watch. Around her waist she wore a thin belt that seemed to have no buckle. She was clothed in an unusual outfit that seemed to change according to what light was shining on it, which admittedly, was not much here. She flashed an almost-smile at him and bade him come to her.

"What's all this?" Jace looked at her outfit more closely as he approached.

"Tools," she said, "to help you do what you must. Observe."

She tapped the device at her wrist, and Jace felt himself shoved back a few feet.

"Woah! What the hell?"

Tora smiled. "A simple manipulation of gravity. If I'd wanted, I could have sent you flying into the wall, but of course, I would not do that." She smiled, and Jace wasn't sure if she was being serious or not. "It is for defensive purposes only," she continued. "We do not attack, we try to never cause harm, but if we are under threat, we can repel an attacker far enough to have the time to flee."

"Okay, cool," Jace said, taking a step toward her again. "What else have you got?"

She touched a point on the belt, and began to rise into the air, in a graceful motion. Jace halted, stunned.

"Are you freaking kidding me?" he threw his arms up. "You can fly with that thing?"

"Again," she answered, "it has to do with the manipulation of gravity. It is a science that humans will unlock eventually, though too late to have any effect on the worsening climate crisis of your century. Not that it would be of much use, anyway. But for us, it allows for quick escapes, and also to get into places that might otherwise be barred to us."

"People in the past have sometimes seen us descend from our craft, though we try not to be spotted," Aereon added. "There are many legends around the world of 'sky people' descending from the clouds. That would be us, with our ships hidden above, out of view."

Jace looked at him. "Is this why abductees see the greys at their windows, even when they're up a floor or two?"

Aereon nodded. "It's the same technology, though their application of it is somewhat different. Some of them make use of it through implants in their bodies that allow them to control the process with their minds."

"That's incredible, but kind of creepy at the same time," Jace said. He looked back to Tora. "What about the suit?"

"It is embedded with luminous threads that can be altered in brightness from nearly complete dark to increasing degrees of illumination," she answered. "It allows the wearer to blend in with the shadows and not be seen."

"It is how we move about at night without detection much of the time," Aereon added. "Of course, where you're going, you'll need some appropriate clothing for the time."

"Wait," Jace grimaced, "you want me to wear stockings and a jester's hat, or something?"

Aereon chuckled and even the stoic Tora smirked. "You really know very little about history," he said.

"Hey, I'm an electrical engineer, not a historian!"

"You'll find that all disciplines are far more intertwined than you might realize," Aereon said. "Ignorance of this fact is perhaps one of the key reasons why the societies in your century are struggling. There was too much partitioning, too much gate-keeping, and various groups were not willing to listen to one another. A lack of an understanding of history inevitably means that the trials of the past will return, often in worse forms, until the lesson is remembered. And what is science without art? What is law without a commitment to compassion and understanding? A lack of understanding and listening between these groups greatly worsened the conditions of your time. In the new world we are building, we will be sure not to make that mistake again."

"Fair enough," Jace said with a nod. "So… do I get to try these out?"

"We have a suit prepared for you already," Tora said.

"Excellent!" Jace clapped his hands together.

"It will take some practice…" she cautioned.

"Eh, I'm ready. Bring it on!"

• • •

"Oof!" Jace lay on his back on the floor. Everything hurt. He looked up to see Tora striding over to him, that smirk on her face broader than before. She reached down to give him a hand up.

"You've fallen seven times," she teased. "Shall we make it eight?"

"You're funny," he grunted as he stood up. "But seriously, what am I doing wrong?"

"You are not centered," she said. "Have you ever practiced any of the Asian martial arts?"

"I took a few months of karate in high school. I wasn't very good at it, though, just ended up getting knocked on my butt most of the time. These days I stick to hiking and golf."

"Ah, but even those pastimes require concentration of a sort, no? In golf, you must stand appropriately, focus to hit the ball with the club, and direct it to go where you want."

"Yeah, I guess."

"And so it is the same with mastering this science. You must direct your intention to your wish, for it is integrated with your thoughts."

"Wait, you mean this little thing," he pointed to the device on his wrist, "can read my mind?"

"It is not sentient, but it responds to your intention. Just as in golf, you intend to hit the ball over a certain trajectory, so here, you must intend that you rise up to a certain height and descend with the same care. Do not let other thoughts interfere with this process."

"Yeah, that's easier said than done," Jace said, looking down at his belt. "Guess I should have paid more attention in those meditation classes my wife signed me up for."

"There is much wisdom in those teachings. You should take up the practice again when you return to your own time."

"I'll keep it in mind, so to speak."

To his surprise, Tora let out a small laugh. "I like you, Jace. There is an earnestness about you that tells me you will be of use."

"Of use? Thanks… I think."

"There is no greater compliment than knowing that you are part of something greater than yourself, and that in endeavouring to change fate, you actually do it."

"That sounded very, um, dark, but hopeful, I guess?"

"I come from a turbulent time."

"Right, yeah, from Scandinavia, right?"

"I was born in the Christian year of 841. My family came from what you know as Norway, but I settled in England by way of the Danish lands."

"Wow, so you're like, a Viking? That's amazing!"

"That's a bit of an oversimplification."

"Still, it sounds incredible! Tell me about it."

"Now is not the time." The coolness of her answer was such that Jace decided not to pursue it further. He sensed she was hiding much about herself, and perhaps had endured great pain. So he let it go. "Come, you must practice until you can raise and lower yourself without injury… and without embarrassing yourself."

The fact that she didn't smile as she said these words made Jace wonder if she was serious or not.

· · ·

"How did you fare?" Aereon asked Jace later as they left the training room.

"Well, I kind of got beat up, to be honest; it's a lot harder than it looks! But I think I have the basics down. I can raise myself up and descend without crashing into the ground, at least, and I learned enough to use the wrist device to repel Tora. The first time I tried it, I shot her halfway across the room. I don't think she was too happy about it!"

"She is a formidable warrior, so perhaps you wounded her pride."

"What's up with her?" Jace pressed.

"What do you mean?"

"What's her story?"

"That is not for me to tell."

"No, I know, but it seems pretty amazing that she went from being born in the ninth century to doing… this" he gestured around with his hand.

"Is it any stranger than your own circumstances?"

Jace sighed and conceded the point. "Not really I guess." He grunted as an ache shot up his back.

"Are you unwell?" Aereon stopped and looked at him.

"Just the workout," Jace said, rubbing his back. "I imagine I'll be in a lot of pain tomorrow."

"We can give you something for the pain, should it be too much to bear," Aereon answered.

"Thanks, I figured you'd have aspirin in the thirty-first century."

"It's a restorative drink, and is far more effective, I assure you. It will not just mask the pain, but will help rapidly heal any injured tissue, so that the source of the discomfort is stopped altogether."

Jace almost stopped. "That's… that's incredible!"

"We have many marvels in this century, not only of technology, but also of mind and spirit. I assure you that you've only seen the smallest portion of them."

"I'm not sure if that's thrilling or kind of scary."

Aereon turned to him. "Perhaps a bit of both?" He smiled and began walking again.

"Where are we going now?"

"To prepare you to meet your family. Do you still want to do it?"

"Yes, um, yes, I do. It's all just so weird, but I feel like I have to, you know?"

"We can postpone the meeting if you wish."

"No, no, I think it's something I need to do. I mean, I'm not sure I want to, but the idea that a part of me is out there that I know nothing about? I couldn't live without knowing who they are. Do they, do they know about me? That I'm here now, I mean?"

"They have been informed."

"And are they like, I don't know, anxious? Do they even want to see me?"

"I'm not aware of what their opinion is of the matter."

"You know, you sound an awful lot like a robot sometimes!"

Aereon turned and gave him a questioning look. "I simply state the truth. I am not unfeeling or uncaring. I promise you that I have the same range of emotions as you do. But perhaps I control them better?"

"Perhaps you do."

"And not knowing what your family's reaction to your presence is, I can hardly speak for them."

"Fair enough. I'm sorry if I implied that you're a, you know, a robot."

Aereon smiled a little. "No offense taken, I assure you. There are worse things that one could aspire to be, I suppose."

"I suppose." Jace took a deep breath. "All right then, lead on."

. . .

Jace waited outside of a door. Or rather he stalled for time. Aereon had left him and told him to enter when he was ready, but that was already five minutes ago? Ten? It was one thing to think about this meeting, but another entirely to go through with it.

"What do I say? How do I act? What if they hate me? What if the kids blame me for the fact they exist at all? Damn it, I can't do this!"

He turned to leave, but something pulled him back. This was no external voice from one of the greys or the others, but a tug from his own conscience.

"If I don't do this, I'll always wonder. And it'll make things more awkward than they already are. Okay. Get it together, Jace, you can do this!"

He took several deep breaths and pressed the small button to the left of the entrance. It opened and his heart raced. He took a few tentative steps in and could see three people in the medium light of the room. The largest (presumably the mother) sat in a chair. She wore a dark blue robe with a hood drawn over her head. Standing beside her were two children, a girl and a boy. As he stepped closer, he could see that they were small, had heads that were a little larger than what he thought was normal, and that their hair was thin on their heads. Their eyes were large, though not as large as the woman's. They stared at him without emotion, each holding one of their mother's hands.

"Um, hi," Jace said, raising one hand in a gesture of greeting, before deciding that he must look ridiculous. He let his hand drop to his side again and stood in silence, hoping that one of them—any one of them—might say something.

"Welcome," said the woman, in a voice that was both human-sounding and somehow otherworldly.

"Thank you," Jace said with a slight nod. "Um, I'm a little out of my depth here. This is pretty awkward, to be honest, so I don't know what I should do, or say, or…"

"I understand," she said with a slight nod. She let go of the boy's hand and reached up to draw back her hood. She looked both human and not. Her eyes were large and almond-shaped, with pupils of amber, and her head was mostly bald with the exception of a few wisps of hair. Her nose was small but visible, and her mouth thin but wider than that of the greys. She looked very much like a blend of the "aliens" he was familiar with and a human woman. Despite her unusual appearance, he was struck by her regal nature and her beauty.

"I am called Ona," she said, with another slight nod of her head.

The word struck Jace as he remembered it from just prior to his abduction. "I… I know," he stammered. He looked at the boy. "And you, you're called…"

"Cam," Ona said. Again, the name came back to him.

"And you?" Jace looked at the girl. "I'm so sorry, but I don't know—or maybe don't remember—your name."

"She is Susan," Ona replied.

"Susan," Jace said. "Wow, just Susan. I love it." He let out a chuckle in spite of himself and felt his eyes sting with tears. "They're both amazing, beautiful, I just, I don't…"

"I understand your emotion and the difficulty that this situation might present," Ona said.

"Are they, are they mine… ours?"

"Indeed," she answered. "They are the product of your genetic material mingled with mine. Conventional reproduction between us—the sex act—would not have been possible; our physical forms are too different. But genetically, we are still compatible with the elder race of humans, and in combining our DNA with theirs, we are creating a new species of human that will be stronger, wiser, and far better adapted to the challenges of the world we are repairing."

"Future humans, eh? This is, it's just incredible. Mind-blowing. I have kids… in another time! Can I, can I talk to them? Do they understand me?"

"Of course," Ona said with more kindness than Jace might have thought he deserved, given his stammering. She whispered something in Susan's ear; she nodded and looked back at Jace before taking a few hesitant steps toward him.

"Hi," he said, kneeling down.

"Are you my father?" she asked in a quiet, child-like voice.

"I guess I am," he said, and those words sparked a response in him. He felt a rush of tears to his eyes and reached up to wipe them away with his sleeve.

"Why do you cry?" she asked.

"I don't know. I'm just, I wasn't expecting this, and I'm really happy to see you, to meet you."

Susan smiled and held out one hand. Jace took it in his. It was small, delicate, tender, fragile. He wanted to scoop her up in his arms right there and hold her, but he held back, quite sure that this would be a breach of some protocol.

"I hope that I can get to know you better, and your mother, over time," he said instead.

Susan smiled. "I would like that… father."

Jace felt another round of tears coming and had to look away. After pulling himself together again, he looked back at her. She stood gazing at him with a faint smile. He returned her smile and looked past her to Ona and Cam. Cam had turned around and had buried his head in Ona's robe.

"Forgive him," Ona said as she stroked his head with her slender fingers. "He is the older of the two, but is still shy, perhaps afraid. It might be too much for him yet."

"I understand," Jace said, standing up. "There's no hurry. He doesn't have to see me, up close I mean, if he doesn't want to."

"Thank you for understanding," Ona said with a nod.

"So, um, I'd love to, I don't know, talk with you in private, if you want. I feel like we should do that, I guess."

Ona again gave him a nod. "When I am free from my duties, we can speak at length, about whatever you wish."

"Good, good, that's great. Um, so I have to meet with Aereon in a bit, and I should probably go do that. I just wanted, you know, to make contact, to see you, to see you all. It's amazing, and I have questions, and I don't even know what I'm feeling right now, so please forgive me if I seem really weird, or rude, and…"

Ona interrupted him with a light laugh. "There is no need to feel discomfort in my presence. What we have done was from necessity, for the greater good. I am grateful to meet you, and hope that we can indeed speak more when the time is right."

Jace felt a surge of relief. "Good, yeah, great, thank you. Really. I'd like that. And we will, we will. Soon?"

"At your convenience."

"Okay, good." He turned back to look down at Susan. "I will see you again, all right? Would you like that?"

She smiled and nodded before turning around and hurrying back to Ona. For the first time since he'd been here, Jace felt a lightness of heart and spirit, unlike anything he'd experienced in a long time.

• • •

"How was your meeting?" Aereon asked Jace later as they sat in what looked like a lounge. Jace ate some food that was simple, but nourishing and satisfying.

"Surreal. Emotional. I don't know. I'm still processing it."

"I understand. It will take some time. But know that your contribution has been for the greater good and will benefit this world in numerous ways."

"My 'contribution.' Heh, I guess that's one way of putting it. Should've tried that as a pick-up line in college. 'Honest! We're contributing to saving the future world!'"

Aereon grinned, but Jace had the sense that it was more out of politeness than any camaraderie, or even understanding of his joke.

"So, what is this?" He changed the subject and pointed at the food on his silver-colored plate. "It's pretty good."

"It is a balanced food, prepared from mushrooms. All the nutrients you need are in it."

"Mushrooms, I should have known. Doesn't really taste all that 'mushroomy' though. I guess that's a good thing?

Don't want everything tasting like everything else. Still, I'm telling you: it could do with some garlic."

"We have many kinds of foods, I assure you," Aeron said. "This is prepared to help those who have made the jump through time to stay healthy and adapt. Were you to spend longer with us, you would discover a nice variety of foods here," he grinned again, "some of which you might even find tolerable."

Jace laughed, almost spitting out his mouthful of processed mushroom whatever-it-was. "You know, I think you're way funnier than you're letting on."

"I have to be, if I'm going to be shepherding around people from the past. What else can one do but see the humor in it?"

"Good point." Jace set aside his plate. "I think that's enough mushroom nutrient thing for now. I don't want to fill up; I'm supposed to go and train more with Tora in a bit. But I need to know more about what I'm doing, how I'll do it."

Aereon nodded. "Tora and I will be with you at all times, nearby if not in your presence. You will wear clothing appropriate to the servant classes of the time, and you will infiltrate the group of noblemen planning to murder the king. It is imperative that this not happen."

"But I'm no spy. How am I going to do that without messing it up, or getting myself killed?"

"You simply need to hear their plans, while serving them food and drink."

"So, I'll be a waiter. Got it."

"At which point, you will return to us with the information," Aereon apparently ignored his latest attempt at levity.

"Okay, and?"

"And at that moment, your role should be complete."

"Wait, that's it? That's all I do? Then… what's the point of me training to use this fancy tech? Hell, what's the point of me even going?"

"You need the training in case something goes wrong."

"And…often do things go wrong?"

"Often enough that people like you need training. This is dangerous work, Jace. Not only is there a risk to those of us venturing into the past, there is also the risk of altering the timeline too drastically. Secrecy is essential at all times."

"So, what if our cover gets blown?"

"We can mask memories, as we do in modern abductions, but the process is not perfect, and in time, the person will begin to recall what really happened."

"Fine, but I still don't quite get why you need me for this. Why doesn't Tora just do it herself? She's obviously way more experienced than me, and probably won't screw it up. I'm pretty sure she can kick my ass, so she'd be a much better choice, right?"

"In this case, the gathering of conspirators is a group of men, fairly rough ones at that, even for nobles. They would not expect to see a woman there at all; it would raise questions and might put her in greater danger."

"Okay, so why not you?"

"My eyes and features give me away as something unusual. I would be a distraction and possibly even the subject of superstitious fear. We need an ordinary-looking human man for the task."

"Oh, I'm 'ordinary.' Okay, I guess I won't be insulted."

"You know what I mean." Aereon seemed almost impatient.

"But I still don't see why you're asking me in particular to do this."

"You have experienced loss of sleep, irritability, confusion, and much more these past few weeks in your own time, yes?"

Jace nodded. "I'm working way too hard."

"That may be so, but there is more to your symptoms than that." Aereon sighed. "Jace, one of the reasons you were chosen for this mission specifically is that you are also a descendant of this king."

The words hit Jace like a sledge hammer. It wasn't the first revelation to do this, but it might have been the biggest.

"Hold on, just a minute! I'm…"

"You are a part of the bloodline of Edward III, illegitimately, of course. But because of that, and because of the danger that Edward II might be killed, that is why you are feeling out of sorts. As this bloodline gets erased from history, all those who descend from him will disappear as well. Your symptoms are the start of this timeline alteration."

"You mean…"

"If we do not stop this murder, and soon, you, like all of his descendants, will be erased from history, and cease to exist."

CHAPTER 7

JACE STEPPED OUT OF THE woods near his home, looking across the field to the row of houses in the distance. True to their word, the humans from the future had returned him to the exact moment that they'd taken him, but why they hadn't just dropped him in his bedroom, he didn't know.

"Maybe they figured the night air would clear my head," he said with a half-chuckle.

He started across the field, taking uneven, hesitant steps, his mind whirling with everything that had happened over... the last day? The last several days? He wasn't sure.

"What does time even mean anymore?"

He paused for a moment a few steps into the field and took a deep breath of the night air. All was quiet and calm, at least on the outside, but he began to experience a sense of dreadful unease growing inside him, coming over him like a wave of pain or nausea. He could feel his body begin to tremble, which grew into a full-blown shake. He sank to his knees and put his hands over his face as tears flooded his eyes. It was all madness, it couldn't be true.

"But I was there," he sobbed. "I saw it all! It's real!"

He gave in and allowed himself time to let it all out, everything he'd been suppressing, everything he'd shoved down into the back of his memory for years. Somehow, it all clicked. A part of him that he'd never understood now made sense. And his stress in recent months, it was clear now. He guessed that his abductors had left him alone so that he could have this moment, experience what he needed to feel on his own. If so, he thanked them for it.

He wasn't sure how long he sat there, alone in the night, but eventually, he gathered himself together and stood up on shaky legs. As he began to make his way home, he reached one hand into his pocket. His keys were right where he'd left them. Aereon and the others hadn't forgotten. Again, he was grateful.

"Three days," he said. "They'll be back here in three days, and then? Whatever the hell I have to do, I'll do. No idea how that's going to work."

He reached his home without incident and crept in, just as he'd done before. Removing his shoes and coat, he snuck upstairs and was pleased to find Sara asleep, just as he'd left her. If she was aware of his coming and going, she didn't show it. Removing his clothes, he climbed into bed and tried to think about everything that had happened. But the more he tried, the more fatigued he became. Perhaps this was a gift from his visitors, as well. Before long, he felt himself drifting off, and he welcomed the deep black of sleep.

. . .

When Jace opened his eyes, it was already sunny outside, and morning was well underway. Sara was up and out of the bedroom, and he was glad to be alone for a minute or two. He sat up and was pleased that he felt rested, more so than he had in weeks, maybe months. Whether it was the release of last night, of integrating his repressed memories back into his waking mind, or if they'd just given him something to help him sleep better, he didn't know.

"Either way, I'll take it."

He got out of bed, threw on his robe, and went downstairs. Sara was sitting at the kitchen table, checking her phone. To his surprise, she seemed happy and less stressed herself.

"Good morning!" she said with a genuine smile.

"Good morning," he answered, smiling back and going to pour himself some coffee. The first sip revealed that it wasn't too hot anymore, but he didn't mind. Coffee was coffee.

"It's so strange," she said, putting her phone down. "I slept better last night than I have in ages. It felt like I got twelve hours. It was amazing!"

"Huh, so did I!" Jace was pleased to hear her say it. "I wonder why that happened?"

"Maybe we both just hit a wall and our bodies said 'enough'? It's been a rough few weeks. I don't know, but whatever it was, I wish I could feel this good every morning."

"Yeah, me too. Hey, we're still doing the trip today, right?" Jace was pleased that he hadn't forgotten about their short overnight trip to the woods up north. He felt sharper all around, and it was an amazing sensation after months of dullness.

"Oh yeah, the kids can't wait. They're out now, doing a bit of last-minute shopping for snacks. I mean, it's only for one night, but it'll be good to go to the cabin again, yeah?"

Jace chuckled, chugging his only-warm coffee. "Yeah, it'll be nice to be outside in the woods for a while, even just overnight."

"Good thing we're both so rested," she said, walking by and giving him a quick kiss on the cheek. "I was kind of dreading it, what with how tired we've both been lately."

"So was I, but I feel great now. I think tonight's exactly what we need."

"Well, they'll be back in a bit, so we should probably shower and get ready." She turned to look at him with a seductive gaze. "My back could use some scrubbing. Just saying…"

Jace's eyes widened a little and he smiled, putting down his coffee mug. "Your wish is my command, my dear."

She took his hand and led him back upstairs.

• • •

"Thanks for this, dad," Grace kissed Jace on the cheek, "even if it's only till tomorrow."

"Of course," Jace hugged her and she darted off upstairs. "Good night!"

The cabin was located in the middle of a dense forest, only an hour's drive north of their home. They'd had a great afternoon, hiking and exploring, and Jace had almost forgotten about his incredible adventure in the future. Almost. He sat on the sofa with Sara, grateful for some alone time.

"This place always amazes me," he said after a moment. "Not far from civilization at all, but it's like a whole different world. Nobody knows you're here, and you can ignore the world, at least for a bit."

"It is nice, isn't it?" Sara snuggled up next to him. "We should come up here more often. Maybe even just the two of us sometimes?"

"I'd like that a lot," he smiled as she drew closer. "This would be a great place to come to in the winter: a bit of snow, a nice fire…"

"Mmmm, that would be cozy. Let's plan on it, then. Sometime in January? We could shuttle Tom and Grace off to my mom's for a weekend. We'll book it when we get home."

Jace drew her even closer and they lapsed into a peaceful doze, the sound of the ticking antique clock lulling them to sleep with its gentle clicks. Jace was so at peace that he almost didn't notice the roaring noise outside at first.

"What the hell was that?" Sara sat up.

Jace was up in an instant and peering out the front window. "Turn the light off."

Sara did so and came to join him. Looking outside, he could see a car and a motorcycle in the light of the moon. They'd driven up the dirt road and parked some distance from the house. Several noisy young men exited the car and two got off the motorcycle. They were laughing, roughing each other up, and being obnoxious. One pulled out a six-pack of beer, and started tossing cans to his friends. They laughed and opened the cans, downing them quickly. Another six-pack was out and passed around soon after.

"Are you kidding me?" Sara's voice dripped with anger. "So now our peace and quiet is going to be interrupted by these idiots?"

"They probably didn't think anyone would be up here. And now that they see us, they probably don't care."

"Mom? Dad? What's going on?" Grace came rushing down the stairs with Tom right behind her.

"Some jerks have decided to park outside and have a party, apparently," Sara said.

"Should we go out and tell them to leave?" Tom asked, looking like he was spoiling for some action.

"No!" Sara commanded. "You'll do no such thing. You're staying inside, no matter what."

Tom put his head down, but didn't say anything else.

"Should we call the police?" Sara asked, turning back to Jace.

"I mean, we could, but they might have a bit of a time finding us. Not even sure they've got GPS out here. That's the only problem with being remote… it's remote!"

He remembered that he wore the small wrist device on his left arm, to practice with when no one else was around. "I think I can handle this."

"What do you mean?" Sara asked with some alarm.

"I'm going to go out there and tell them to leave. I think I can convince them."

Jace, no! There's what... six of them? What if they're already drunk? What if they get violent? What if they have guns?"

"Trust me, I'll be fine." Jace was already making for the door, when he turned and said to the others, "Everyone wait here. I got this. I'll have them out of here in no time."

Before his family could protest, he opened the door, strode out, and closed it behind him. He took a breath, focused for a moment on his wrist, and then began to walk toward the group. His heart raced.

You'd better know what you're doing!

"Hey guys!" he shouted before he could think about it and turn around. A couple of them looked up at him, obviously surprised that anyone was out here, even though the cabin lights had been on. "We're trying to sleep here. Would you mind taking your partying somewhere else? I've got kids."

"We come up here all the time, dude," one said to him, throwing his empty beer can on the ground. "We're just having some fun, not hurtin' anyone."

"Didn't say you were," Jace answered as he drew closer. "Honestly, I'm cool with you doing whatever you want; I used to do stuff like this, too. But like I said, we'd like to get to sleep soon, so if you could take it somewhere else, just for tonight, that'd be great."

"I mean, this ain't your property, right?" Another one said, taking a good chug of his can.

"No," Jace answered, getting annoyed. "But it's not yours either. We paid to be here for the night."

"So that makes you special, then?" The second young man said.

"Nope, but it does mean we have a right to enjoy the place."

"Well," said the first in a sarcastic tone, "we're not on the property, we're in the road, so as long as we stay here, there's nothing you can do about it." His friends laughed.

"I could call the cops," Jace threatened.

"Oooh, I'm scared!" another joked, eliciting more laughter.

"Look guys," Jace said, holding up his hands, his attention focused on his left wrist. "I don't want to fight, really. I'm cool with you being out here, but come on, just be reasonable."

An empty beer can went whizzing past his head, followed by a chorus of more laughter.

Jace sighed. "You really don't want to do this, believe me."

"What are ya gonna do, dude?" another spoke up after a loud belch. "We got plenty more cans."

"I'm sure you do," Jace said, now angry. "Come here and try that again, only closer."

The young men looked at each other in surprise, and then laughed again. The one who threw the empty can picked up an unopened can and stepped forward.

"Okay man," he said with a grin. "But this one might hurt a bit more." More laughter.

"It'll never hit me," Jace taunted.

"Woah, that's a big claim, dude," his nemesis said, clutching his can and preparing to throw it.

"Well, come here and try, you little jerk."

The young man scowled. "I'm gonna make this hurt!"

He started to run toward Jace, bringing up his hand to throw his makeshift weapon. Jace stood his ground, his attention focused on the device on his wrist.

Just a few more steps.

As his would-be attacker drew his arm back to throw, Jace thrust his left arm forward, his thoughts and intention set on the device.

Please work!

He felt a vibration in the device and then a pulse, like a wave of sound, but silent, as it washed over his hand and shot forward. It struck the young man head-on and knocked him back at least ten feet, sending him sprawling on the ground and the beer can flying away into the darkness.

"What the hell?" one of the others cried out. Two more of them took tentative steps toward Jace, while his first assailant was still prone on the ground, looking more confused than hurt.

"Okay, who's next?" Jace taunted, emboldened by the effectiveness of his futuristic defense.

"You think you're really funny, eh?" One of them shouted back as he hurled his can at Jace. Jace brought up his arm and with barely a thought and shot a repulsing beam at the missile, sending it at back at the thrower, and causing him to scramble to miss it as it sailed by.

"Yeah, I'm hilarious," Jace said. "But you? You're all just idiots. Now get out of here before I decide to do some real damage."

The rest of the group hesitated, but looking at one another, they seemed to get their courage back. "He can't take out all of us, whatever he's doing," one of them said, probably as much for his own assurance as anything else.

"Well, we'll see," Jace said in a calm voice as they approached him as a group. All six now moved in on him, looking angry and determined. He almost wanted to laugh, but he held it in. Again, he waited. They loomed before him, making fists and threatening with their beer cans. He couldn't help himself and let out a guffaw. This only made them angrier, and they broke into a run. A moment later they regretted it.

Jace let out another blast from his wrist device, not holding back this time. The force struck them head-on, knocking all six back ten feet or more, sending them crashing into each other and their vehicles.

"We can keep going," Jace called out, "or you can get out of here and leave us alone. Your choice."

He waited for their reaction. They slowly gathered themselves together, but no one approached him.

"I'm going to give you thirty seconds to leave," Jace said. "Or the next blast is really going to hurt, and I'm probably gonna go after your car. I'll bet I could knock it several feet into the air and turn it over. Should we find out?"

"Screw this, man!" One of them yelled. "I'm out of here! You can stay if you want, but I'm not letting him hurt my car." He scrambled into the driver's seat and started the engine. The others followed and jumped into the car or onto the motorcycle. They made a hasty turnaround and in less than thirty seconds, they'd sped off into the darkness, leaving a few beer cans in their wake.

Jace smiled. The smile became a laugh. He looked at his wrist and patted the slender band around it. His mirth turned to worry though, as he heard Sara's voice behind him. He closed his eyes.

"She probably saw everything. She knows."

• • •

"Jace, what the hell was that?" Sara motioned out toward where their intruders fled. "What did you do?"

He turned to look back at her. "It's nothing, Sara. I just scared them off, that's all."

"You're lying, please stop it! I saw what you did to those guys with my own eyes. It made no sense at all. They went flying into the air. Now, what is going on?"

Jace sighed and looked down, then back at her. "Okay, fine, here it is, the truth. Humans from the future are visiting us in saucer-shaped craft, but we think they're aliens. They're trying to repopulate and regrow the Earth of the thirty-first century. I even have a separate family there made from DNA I gave to them in college. Now, they need me to go back in time and stop the murder of a medieval English king, because one of his descendants is an important scientist who won't be born for a few centuries. Oh, and I'm an indirect descendant of the king too. He's already been murdered in a historical event that wasn't supposed to happen. So, I have to go back with a team of others and stop it, or I'll be erased from existence, which, incidentally, is why I've been so restless and stressed lately. I'm starting to disappear from the timeline."

She stared at him, speechless.

"Sara?"

She shook her head and her eyes filled with tears. "You know, I really thought things were getting better. We both woke up feeling so great today and we had this cabin trip to look forward to. Hell, we even took a shower together! When was the last time that happened? And now this," she motioned again with her hand. "Now you're making up some BS story. Or maybe you really do believe it, I don't know. Maybe you *are* losing your mind. Oh God…" she turned away.

"Sara, please. Listen," He reached out to her, but she pulled away as soon as his hand touched her shoulder.

"I don't know what's going on with you," she glanced back at him, tears rolling down her cheeks, "but you've got two kids back in that cabin who deserve better than the way you're behaving. If you won't get your life together for me, at least do it for them!"

"I have, I am!" he protested. "Look, I know it sounds nuts…"

"Yeah, you think?"

"But I'm not lying."

"No, you're probably not. I think you really do believe whatever crazy stories you've come up with. Oh Jace, don't you see? Can't you realize what a mess you are?" She turned back toward him. "I love you, but I can't keep doing this. If you're not going to take this stress seriously and get help, I mean *real* help, then I can't be here. And they can't, either." She pointed to the cabin behind her.

"Look," Jace pleaded, "I can prove everything I just said, no matter how ridiculous it sounds."

"And how are you going to do that? Are you going to invite your little green friends over for coffee some afternoon? Introduce them to the family?"

"No, look," he held up his wrist. "This device, it can control gravity. You saw what it did. How on Earth would I have something like this if I was just making up stories?"

"I don't know," she sighed. "Maybe it's some experimental tech from work. You guys are always working on cutting edge stuff, right?"

"No, we're nowhere near this. No one is. This is beyond anything that science is capable of right now, trust me. It came to me from the far future."

Sara threw up her arms. "Jace, do you know how you sound? Do you have any idea how crazy that is? I don't know what that… thing is, but there has to be a better explanation than, 'it's from the future!'"

A white glow appeared in the tree line.

"Oh great!" Sara exclaimed. "You probably just pissed them off, and now they're back with more of their friends."

"No, no that's not it," Jace shuddered. He knew that light. It was the same one that had beckoned him into the trees outside their home. He took a step toward it.

"Jace, no, don't!" Sara warned.

"It's okay," he said, turning to assure her. "This is important. If they're here now…"

"If who's here?" Sara demanded. "Damn it, Jace, I'm getting really tired of all of this…"

A silhouette appeared at the edge of the tree line. Jace recognized it immediately, a human-shaped figure that moved with an elegance not often seen among people in his own time.

"Aereon," he half smiled.

"What?" Sara asked. "Who is that? What's going on?"

"Wait," he answered.

"Jace, I don't like this."

"No, really, it's okay. It'll all be fine." *I hope.*

"Aereon," Jace said again, in a louder voice, addressing his new friend. He took a few more steps forward. "Good to see you again. I wasn't expecting you back quite so soon."

Aereon came into view. He was wearing a light reflecting suit, exactly like Tora's, and the kind that Jace knew had been prepared for him. He didn't smile, but he did hold up one hand in a greeting as he strode toward them.

"Jace," Sara said, gripping his arm as if to hold him back. "What is going on?"

Aereon walked straight up to them and nodded his head, first at Jace, and then at Sara. "My apologies, my friend, and my apologies to you, lady. I wish we could have met under better circumstances."

"What's going on?" Jace asked, taking Sara's hand in his.

"The situation is worse than we feared," Aereon answered. "The timeline is coming unraveled in unexpected places, which means that we must go now. We cannot wait even a few more days."

Jace sighed.

"Jace?" Sara looked at him. "Seriously, what is happening?"

"Again, I am sorry," Aereon addressed her. "You have no doubt seen the function of the device he wears at his wrist? We gave it to him for practice. If he has told you anything about us at all, I can confirm that it's true."

Sara looked back and forth between him and Jace for a moment. "Is this some kind of joke? Are you a work buddy? What, are you punking me with stories about time travel? Because it's not funny, not even a little bit!"

"There is no deception here, I promise you," Aereon said, holding up both hands, palms facing her. "Jace is special, and we need him. He has an important role to play in re-setting a timeline gone badly wrong. Believe me, we would not normally want to involve you, but it is a matter of some urgency and so our secrecy must be sacrificed in this case. We need him to come with us now, but we will return him to you at this very moment when we have completed our task. It will be almost as if he never left."

"Look," Jace said, turning to her and taking both of her hands. "I promise I'll explain everything when I get back, but this... this is important. I don't understand it all, either, but it's something I've got to do. A whole lot of people are depending on me. Reality might be depending on me."

"Jace, please, whatever is happening, you don't have to do anything you don't want to."

"I do, though, that's the problem. It affects me personally. It's complicated. But if everything goes as planned, I'll come walking out of those woods in a minute or so, and then I'll tell you everything."

"And if everything doesn't go as planned?"

"That's… not an option. Please Sara, trust me on this. I'm not lying to you and I don't want to lose you, ever. I have to go now, but I'll be right back. I will!"

He squeezed her hands and stepped back. The look of hurt and mistrust on her face haunted him, and he fought against the urge to stay, to tell Aereon that he couldn't go.

"I am sorry," Aereon said, "but he speaks the truth, and he will return to you momentarily." He gave her another nod of his head and turned to walk back into the woods.

"Fine." Sara threw her hands up. "Go save the world, or whatever. But I expect you back here in a few minutes with the truth, all of it."

"And you'll get it, I promise. I love you."

"I love you, too. Don't make me regret that."

"Never."

Blowing a kiss to her, he turned and ran to catch up with Aereon. After a minute, he could see a glow in the forest, that of the time craft.

"So this is it, huh?"

"It is. We've brought your suit and your necessary clothing. Good work with your wrist device, by the way. I doubt those young men will venture back up here again any time soon."

"It was pretty satisfying, it must be said."

"Just remember, it is for defense. We are not to attack, much less harm, anyone."

"Understood. Tora was pretty clear on that. Is she here?"

"She is with us, as are three greys who will pilot the ship and pull us through the time stream."

"Is it going to be another bumpy ride?"

"Undoubtedly."

Jace sighed. "All right let's get on with it, then. Next stop: merry old England!"

Aereon gave him a quick glance. "It's not very merry where we're going, I'm afraid."

CHAPTER 8

"I HAVE A QUESTION... ABOUT this whole 'changes to the timeline' thing." Jace sat in a simple contoured chair in an unadorned and tan-colored circular room inside the craft. If this was a piloting or command center, it sure didn't look like it. Aereon sat in a chair next to him on his right. A third, empty chair, presumably for Tora, was to the right of Aereon's.

"I can attempt to answer," Aereon replied, "but I make no guarantees that I have the knowledge. Time is a mercurial and strange thing."

"Yeah, that's what I figured," Jace sighed. "But anyway, here it is: if something changes in the past, doesn't it just create alternate timelines? Like if I went back in time and killed Hitler as a boy—not that I'm saying I should do that—but if I did, wouldn't that just create a new reality where that was the case, but have no effect on our own?"

"It is a good question, and the best answer I can give you is that the physics is complex. It is indeed possible that new realities are created when events are altered, but we think that a high amount of energy needs to be involved for the event to birth an entirely new reality. We are still studying this phenomenon, and we haven't unraveled that mystery yet."

"Okay, I guess that makes sense, but you also said that this murder of this king has already happened, even though it hasn't, really, or it has, but it's not yet known in my time. Why not?"

"When a smaller event such as the removal of a pivotal figure takes place, the timeline is altered but not fractured. It will change what came after it, but not instantaneously. Think of it like dropping a small stone into a pond. The splash is the altering event, but its effect will ripple outward from the incident. So, the effects of the change will ripple out across time gradually. This is why you didn't disappear right away when the new event happened, but instead felt ill for a few months. Your form was aware that something had occurred. But as the ripple gets closer in time to you, it will have a more dramatic effect on your body and mind, which is why we need to attend to this issue now."

"Again, okay, but how did this change even happen? If Edward wasn't murdered until later on, why would there be a sudden change unless… hang on."

Aereon looked down, as if embarrassed.

"Is this something your people did? Did you screw up something in that era, and now you need me to fix it?"

Aereon looked up at him. "That is perhaps an oversimplification, but, essentially, there is truth to your statement."

"Truth to my statement? Oh damn it, I don't believe this! So you all went and did something, messed up events, and you've accidentally started erasing people from history. And now me, one of those people, needs to go fix your mess?"

"You're not going alone."

Jace put his face in his palms and shook his head. "Unbelievable. Actually, no, it's totally believable. What did you do?"

"It had to do with collecting DNA samples. A team of greys was going about the business, as they can be quite discreet, but they were seen, and it set in motion other… regrettable events, leading to a renewed interest in a conspiracy to kill King Edward. But if we can set it right, that anomaly won't matter and will be lost to history. Any other events that might come out of it will be too small to have any effect on the timeline."

"You know," Jace looked up. "I should tell you to turn around and drop me right back where I was."

"If we did that, you would cease to exist before the next morning of that time."

Jace let out a frustrated sigh. "I don't like feeling like I'm being strong-armed into fixing something."

"It is not our intention to force you, but you must understand the consequences of what is happening."

"Consequences that *you* brought about!"

"You have been involved with us, for a long time in your life."

"And I didn't even know that, until you wanted me to."

"Until it was necessary."

"Again, because of something you screwed up!"

"We can argue about this, or we can resolve to correct it and sort out differences later," Tora said as a previously-unseen door slid open and she entered the room, taking her seat next to Aereon. She was dressed in the same suit she'd worn while training Jace, and wore her belt and wrist device.

"Glad to see you're ready," Jace said, though he was in fact, glad to see her.

"This is not a holiday," she answered coldly.

"Okay," Jace paused. "So what happens now?"

In answer, the door opened again and three greys entered. Once more, Jace found it difficult to focus on them, as if they were deliberately dulling his senses to perceiving them. He could only make out their forms and movements in his peripheral vision; when he stared at them, he only saw a grey blur. From what he could tell, the three of them set about touching various places on the wall, which illuminated those points, and made them seem to reach out to each other, almost like a neural network connecting. He was reminded of what Aereon had said about using life integrated into these crafts. It was ingenious, even beautiful, if somehow a little unnerving.

"Am I going to feel all disoriented again?" he asked.

"Probably," was all that Tora would say.

Jace felt a gentle rumbling and heard a low hum. "So, we're lifting off?"

No one answered.

"Fine, I'll just sit here and twiddle my thumbs." He rolled his eyes.

He was startled by a jolt as the craft seemed to surge forward and upward, and yet, while the ship was moving, he felt oddly insulated from the movement, even more so that he might have felt on an airplane.

"Still haven't figured out how to fix that, eh?" Jace quipped.

"We are bound by the laws of physics," Aereon answered, "even if we bend them from time to time."

The craft seemed to accelerate and then slow, but it didn't feel to Jace like a normal slowing.

"What's happening?" he asked, not alarmed but not at ease.

"We are beginning to surge through time," Aereon answered, still looking ahead.

Jace felt a sudden movement to the left, as if the craft were changing directions.

"We are calibrating our position," Aereon went on. "The earth will not be in the same physical place as it is in this time, so we have to compensate for that. The farther away in time we go, the more complex that calculation is."

"And if you miscalculate?"

"We end up in space."

"Oh. And is this craft equipped to handle that?"

"Not especially, no."

"Great."

The craft moved again, farther to the left.

"We were going pretty fast there, it felt like," Jace said after a moment's silence. "How did we make a sharp turn like that at that speed?"

"We are actually warping time, not distance," Aereon said, looking at him at last. "This is why some observers of our craft claim that they make impossible directional shifts mid-flight. We're not actually going very quickly, but observers are given the illusion of high speed right angle turns. This would be similar to speeding up a film."

"Ah, so that's why some air force pilots have reported UFOs doing things that they shouldn't be able to do making crazy right-angle turns and such. You're getting ready to make time jumps."

"Exactly."

Jace sat in silence for a while, watching (as best he could) the three greys, who seemed to be making complex calculations and communicating with each other telepathically. They were so alien and strange to him, and yet on some level, he found himself envying them.

"We are ready," Tora announced.

Aereon looked again at Jace. "Sit with your hands in your lap and relax. If you simply let go, there should be no need to worry about what's to come."

"Uh, what is to come, exactly?"

"Turbulence. You've felt it before, when we brought you to our time."

Almost at once, the ship jolted forward again, and Jace felt himself pushed back into his seat.

"The gravitational force equivalent will increase briefly," Aereon announced. "Remain calm."

"Sure, no problem," Jace answered. "Just knowing that if we miss, we'll get shot into space makes me feel so much better."

"It's never happened… to my knowledge," Aeron said.

"Again, I feel so much better knowing that."

Jace wasn't sure if this trip was easier, or if he was simply more used to it, or perhaps the ship was of better quality, but the process seemed less jarring this time. After a few more thrusts of turbulence and shaking, all seemed still again.

"Was that it?"

"Are you surprised?"

"A bit, yeah."

"You needn't be. This was a fairly easy jump to make, considering that we've been to the time in question before. We knew exactly where and when we were going."

"Right, when you screwed things up."

Aereon didn't answer.

Tora closed her eyes, and seemed to be receiving some communication in her mind. After a few moments of concentration, she opened them again and turned to her companions. "They have informed me that the jump was successful."

"So, we're here," Jace added.

Tora nodded. "Yes, welcome to the year 1310."

• • •

Jace and Tora stood in a small woodland, not unlike the one behind his own home back in the twenty-first century. Only, the view before them could not have been more different. Jace saw a walled castle, not huge, but impressive enough, with a retinue of guards and a flurry of people going in and out of the front gate at the wall. The sun was setting and the time seemed to be autumn, judging by the chill in the air and the falling leaves.

"So, I need to go in there," Jace said, watching as a line of people made their way to the gate. Most were admitted, but a few seemed to be turned away.

"You and I both, yes," Tora answered.

Jace looked at her. It was strange seeing her now attired in the garb of the fourteenth century, as was he. It was plain and unadorned, nothing like the colorful jester's outfit he'd worried they might make him wear. That was something, at least. He wore his lightweight suit under these clothes, along with his belt and wrist device. The medieval clothing covered them all just fine.

He chuckled. "I feel like I'm going to a LARPing event, only it's real."

"And the danger is real," Tora warned him. "Do nothing rash, and without our leave. We have a plan for this. Follow it, and we will succeed."

"Right, I know. I'm just supposed to listen and communicate back to you through this ear thingie what I've heard." He tapped the ear with the implant.

"Do you think you can do that?"

Jace couldn't tell from her expression if she were being serious or sarcastic. "I'll manage. It's my existence that's on the line, after all."

Without another word, she started out of the trees and toward the dirt road that led to the castle walls.

"So, why do they want to murder him, this king?" Jace asked.

"Edward has a favorite, Piers Gaveston, one that he spends all his time with. The king dotes on him, gives him favors, titles, and money. Several other nobles hate Gaveston, and resent the king giving him all that attention."

"Why does the king like this Gaveston guy so much?"

Tora turned to him with an almost sarcastic look. "Why do you think?"

"Huh? Oh. Oh! So they're…"

"Indeed, and it's not an acceptable relationship to have, when he is supposed to be fathering an heir."

"Wow, okay, it all makes sense now."

They walked on for a short time, drawing nearer to the castle.

"So we're back closer to your own time, eh?" Jace tried to make some lighter conversation.

"Not especially." Tora kept her eyes forward and her pace brisk.

"Well, okay, five hundred years later, right? But still closer than the thirty-first century."

"What is your point?"

"Nothing, just, I'd like to know more about you… if, you know, you're willing to share."

Tora stopped and looked at him, as if measuring his words and thinking about her response.

"My parents came from Norway but were murdered by a rival settlement in Denmark when I was nine. I was made a slave and brought to northern England, where I then lived and served. When I was nineteen years old, I found myself in a forest not unlike the one we just landed in. I was allowed to go and forage by that age. I came upon a group of greys, and was overpowered by them. I thought they were elves or trolls, or some such, but when they reached out to me, to my mind, they saw something in me. It seemed that they pitied me and they asked if I wished to accompany them back to their world. I assumed I was being taken to Alfheim or Vanaheim, to Freya and Freyr, so of course, I said yes. It was only after we'd arrived in the future that I understood they were something very different. But I chose to stay and to learn and to assist them in their work, and I've been doing it for ten years now. Is that everything you need to know?"

Jace stared at her in shock, his mouth open. As she turned to resume her stride, he couldn't think of anything to say in response.

"Listen," he finally spoke up as he hurried to catch up to her. "I'm, I'm sorry. Really. I didn't know and I wasn't trying to make you feel bad or uncomfortable, I promise. I was just trying to be friendly, you know, get to know you a little better?"

"We have an important task to do," she answered, looking ahead to the line of people. "We may socialize afterward, if we are successful, and if we fail, you will not be here to ask me questions, anyway."

"Wow, well that's one way to look at it, I suppose."

She stopped abruptly and glared at him. "Is there another way of looking at the situation? One that I do not know about? If we fail, you vanish, along with many others and the future changes. And not for the better."

Jace sighed. "Okay, fine, I get it. Let's get this done. No friendly talk until afterward."

They made their way to the back of the line, which by now had diminished; only a handful of travelers waited in front of them. The sky was growing darker, and the air was already colder than when they'd arrived. Three more people in front of them were let in, while two others were denied. When they protested, they were threatened with swords, which made them stop arguing. Jace watched as they skulked off into the countryside.

"I wonder why they weren't let in?" he mused aloud.

"They probably had nothing of value to offer," Tora said, in a quieter voice.

"And we do?"

She almost smiled at him. "Trust me."

It was their turn to approach the guards. Jace found that his heart raced and his throat was dry. For a moment, he feared this whole plan would be ruined and they would be run off, or worse, arrested. His body shook as he and Tora approached the gate.

"Werthurgh wende ye?" the guard said.

"Uh, what?" Jace had a moment of panic, and tried to shoot an alarmed look at Tora.

"Wethrugh? Speke!"

Jace felt something vibrate at his wrist.

"Pax." Tora held up one hand. "We cometh here upon the request of the baron, to attend on his fellows for their supper this night.

"Why are you here so late?" the guard demanded.

"It could not be helped," she answered. "We were delayed. You know how it can be traveling these roads." She smiled while he looked at her with suspicion.

Jace nodded. "There were wolves and… bears. Problems."

Tora shot him an angry look.

The guard looked back and forth between them for a moment and rubbed his head as if it hurt.

"Get on in with you then, and don't cause trouble. If the lord wants to punish you, it's out of my hands."

"Thank you," Tora nodded.

"Thank you," Jace imitated. And with that, they were inside. They rounded the corner and headed to one side to stand by the wall and survey the inner courtyard. There was a tower complex in the distance that many people were going in and out of, and guards seemed to mill about, almost looking bored.

"Wolves and bears?" she whispered in fury.

"Well, I don't know, I'm not a historian!"

"Exactly, so shut up!" she stormed off in front of him, heading for one of the tower entrances. "And keep up!"

"So what the hell happened back there?" he asked, running to her side again. "Why didn't I understand him at first?"

"Your translator was calibrating the language. It sometimes takes a few moments in a new time setting. Be glad it didn't take longer."

"Okay fine, but what happened after that?"

"I opened his mind to suggestion, which made him agreeable to our words. It's another feature of the wrist device, which you have not yet learned to use."

"Woah, like a Jedi mind trick kind of thing? That's incredible!"

She shot an annoyed look at him. "I have no idea what you're talking about. Let's go!"

. . .

They reached the entrance of the tower and were immediately stopped by a guard in chain mail, holding a spear. "State your business."

"We are part of the help tonight for the meal," Tora spoke before Jace could say anything. "I am in the kitchen and he is a server."

The guard eyed them with suspicion. "You're late."

"Indeed. We already explained this at the front gates. He was content to let us through."

Jace wondered if she was pulling the same mind trick on this guard. And after a moment, he nodded and stood to one side.

"Get on in then, and do your duties with haste, or risk a flogging."

She nodded, and Jace imitated her motion, as they made their way into the torch-lit stone corridor that ran to the left and right.

"The kitchen is down here," she pointed to the left. "We'll go there and blend in. Act like we've been there all along."

"Won't someone notice?"

She shook her head. "They have been very busy preparing food for several hours and will likely be grateful for the help. Once in there, you will take up jugs of wine and prepare to serve those gathered in the hall."

"The nobles who are planning on assassinating the king?"

"Shhhh!" Tora darted her glance around them, and then nodded. "They will strike tomorrow, after the king arrives. They might wait for cover of darkness, or they might not. Once we know what they have planned, we will have a day to counteract it. Just get that information and bring it back to us."

"They're probably not going to talk about it in front of 'lowly servants' like me."

"Of course not, that is why you must hide nearby and listen."

"Oh great, thanks for telling me that slightly important detail just now!"

She let out an exasperated sigh and took hold of his arm. "Come!"

She led him into a large kitchen area, and Jace was pretty sure she knew exactly where they were going. She'd either been here before or had a map or something. He wanted to ask her about it, but given that she was already annoyed with him, and they had to pretend to be part of the servant group, he let it go. The chamber was lit by candles and a roaring hearth fire, near which various kinds of meat were roasting on spits. A stew boiled in a large iron pot, and servants were preparing other foods, baking breads, and milling about. Jace was surprised that the food smelled appealing, not at all what he worried it would be like. Tora conversed with an older woman who nodded. They looked over at Jace, and he tried not to meet their glance. In a moment, Tora came back to him and took him to one side.

"You will serve wine tonight. It will be a good chance to listen to what they say. Yes, they will dismiss you before they speak of their true plans, so you will need to find a place to hide so that you can hear more."

"I'm still not thrilled about this plan."

"Your level of excitement is not relevant."

"You really don't understand sarcasm, do you?"

Tora said nothing else, but led him to the adjacent room where wine jugs were kept. Again, she conversed with an older woman, who nodded and pointed to a row of clay jugs on the table. "The meal is about to begin," she said to him. "Hurry up and take one of these, fill their cups and return. Do it again. And again. Do it for as long as they request wine. The more drunk they get, the more they are likely to reveal."

"This should be really fun," Jace muttered. Tora shot him a look to let him know she'd heard him, and not to mouth off again. He nodded to the woman, took up a jug and went down the corridor to where the hall awaited, still convinced that this was all a very bad idea.

• • •

The table in the hall was not as large as he had expected. A few scraps of food already rested on it, but he knew there would be a lot more courses brought out soon. Six men sat around it, with two empty chairs, one tipped over. They were not wearing armor and had no weapons with them, not that they would. But if these were noblemen, they didn't look particularly wealthy, or especially clean. They were engaged in conversation with each other, and didn't even acknowledge him.

Right, am I supposed to do anything, say anything, or do I just walk up to the table and start pouring?

He decided to be bold, stride forward, and begin serving. Without saying a word, one of the men thrust his arm out, his hand holding an empty goblet. Jace poured wine until his goblet was nearly full. The man took a drink from his cup without so much as a word.

You're welcome, jerk!

Another man, and then another, repeated the motion, and Jace hurried between them to make sure that their cups were filled again.

"Be quicker about it, fool!" the man who seemed to be leader snapped. "We are thirsty and have much work ahead of us. This is no mere gathering for enjoyment."

Jace nodded and stepped back, deciding it was best to say nothing and not arouse suspicions. And so he stood, on and off for the next hour, as food was brought in, the wine flowed and the men became more loose-lipped. Their table manners were appalling, their attitudes even more so, and Jace wondered how such revolting people had risen to the top of this society to rule it. He then remembered that it was all hereditary.

Food and wine came and went, while Jace and another wine server were always on hand as new jugs were brought to them to replace the empty ones. He tried on more than one occasion to hear what they spoke of, but it all seemed trivial.

Come on, get to it!

He'd been staring around the hall, looking for a place to hide. A few corners, including one not far from the main doorway, were not lit by the flames, and provided good shadows, though he doubted he could hide well within them. At last, the men dismissed the servers, and Jace left with the others. As he walked back down the corridor, Tora took hold of his sleeve and pulled him into an alcove.

"What did you see?"

"There are a few corners that are dark, but I'll never get to one of them without those guys seeing me."

"You are forgetting what you wear." Again, she almost smiled.

"What? Oh, of course."

"Take off your clothes, quickly!" she commanded.

"You know, usually someone has to buy me a drink before they get to say that."

Tora glared at him.

"All right, all right!" Jace removed his medieval garb and stood in his shadow suit, marvelling at how well it obscured him, even in this partially lit space.

"Now go, quickly!" Tora ordered. "Slip into the nearest shadows. If you move with speed, they will not notice you."

"Huh. Easy for you to say."

Jace obeyed her and made his way back toward the hall, his heart pounding, and sweat dotting his brow. He swallowed just before stepping back into the hall. He could see the men were now huddled closer together. With a deep breath, he stepped into the room and darted to the left and into the shadows of the corner. One man looked toward him, a suspicious expression on his face.

"What?" said his companion.

"I thought I saw something. In the shadows over there." He pointed toward Jace, who panicked

"You've had too much wine, Stephen," friend laughed. "You're seeing demons or little folk now!"

The first man shook his head and turned away. Jace breathed a sigh of relief.

It works!

"Enough!" ordered the leader. "We must be quick. The plan has changed."

Jace's ears pricked up.

"Why?" asked another. "What's happened?"

"My spies have told me that the runt and his plaything will be arriving tonight, instead of tomorrow, and with only a small party in attendance. He wants to travel unseen, thinking it will be safer for him and Gaveston." The lead man lowered his voice.

Jace's eyes widened.

"So what does that mean?" whispered another.

"It means, you dung sack, that we will ride out to meet them tonight. We will attack and leave none alive. It will seem to be the work of brigands and highwayman, and none will suspect us, because we will disperse after we strike. I will have my men contact you in the days afterward. Edward will be mourned, and a new king will be made."

"But who will it be?"

The lead man glared. "Edward I had other children! It could be Thomas of Brotherton, or Edmund of Woodstock. Hell, it could even be bloody John Balliol of Scotland for all I care. The point is that we remove Edward II from the board, once and for all. No one need know what we've done, and we can restore England's greatness!"

"When will they arrive here?" another asked through a gulp from his wine cup.

"Perhaps two hours after compline, so we must move quickly. We will ride out, two by two and head off in different directions to lower suspicions. We will circle back to the far side of the wood yonder, where my guard of twenty will meet us, and then we will make for the road. Edward is traveling light and small, since he wishes to arrive in secret. It will be the last thing he ever does! Come, prepare yourselves!"

With a quiet cheer, the six men stood and with handshakes and slaps on the back, they left the hall. Jace waited until they were all gone before trying to contact Tora.

Tora! Tora, come in! He projected his thoughts, hoping somehow that it would work.

"I am right here," she said popping her head around the entrance. "What did you learn?"

"It's bad, really bad. That assassination that was going to happen tomorrow? Well, it's happening tonight. Edward is coming here in secret, like now. That's why they were able to kill him and mess up the timeline. They're going to attack Edward's party out on the road, kill them all and make it look like bandits did it. Oh, and their leader's got like twenty more of his own soldiers coming with him. Great news, eh?"

"No, no it is not!" Tora snapped, and Jace was sorry that she took his remark to be humorous. "We cannot stop this. We cannot fend off more than twenty men without there being serious consequences to the timeline. Even if we could kill them, the effects would be disastrous."

Jace thought about it for a moment and an idea came to him. "We won't have to. I have an idea. Tell Aereon and the greys to get the craft ready." He motioned to the corridor. "Come on!"

CHAPTER 9

JACE DASHED OUT INTO THE cold night, looking around in haste. The courtyard was mostly empty now, except for two of the conspirators on horseback, riding side-by side to the gate. They were allowed to pass and then the guards once again closed up behind them.

"Jace!" Tora hissed. "What are you doing?"

He stopped and surveyed the scene. "Damn it!" he whispered, as Tora came up behind him. "We're not going to get out that way. They'll want to know why we're going, when we're probably not even supposed to be out here."

"We cannot fight them, and even if we could, it would allow time for the conspirators to get away," she said.

"It's not the only way out of here." He looked up at the wall. "It's not that high, and we can deflect gravity to get over it, right? Right?"

Tora nodded. "I suppose. It should be manageable."

"And if we do it farther away from the light, we won't be seen, especially not in these suits, yeah?"

"Fine, as long as you are sure. We didn't have a lot of time for training. And you weren't very promising, it must be said."

"Oh, thank you so much for the vote of confidence."

She rolled her eyes and started toward the wall, to a place unlit by torchlight. "Follow my actions and you shall be fine."

She broke into a run and tapped a point on the front of her belt. She rose into the air, and sure enough, cleared the wall and disappeared over the other side. Jace watched in admiration and prepared to follow.

"Okay, man, you've got this."

Talking a deep breath, he exhaled and broke into a run, noting the exact place where Tora touched her belt and rose into the air. A few more steps. A few more.

He pressed the spot on his belt, half expecting to stumble forward and fall flat on his face, but to his amazement, he rose up, just as she had done. The trajectory of his ascent followed hers almost exactly, and he reveled in the exhilaration of soaring through the air, over the wall, and descending to the ground outside. His descent was even and slowed as he neared the ground, letting him land gently, ten feet or so away from Tora.

"Not a bad first attempt," she said almost with a smile. "At least you have no broken limbs."

"One of these days, you're going to be genuinely proud of me."

"I will await that hour with anticipation. Now what are we doing? I have contacted Aereon. The craft is ready."

"I'll explain as we go. Come on!"

He started off in a jog toward the woods, glad to see that no one else was out now, and with their suits, they would not be spied by the guards. In the far distance under a waxing moon, he could see a pair of horses disappearing over the hillside. Increasing his pace, he was not surprised to see Tora overtake him and run past him.

"Come along, keep up!" she ordered. "And tell me what you have planned. I want to hear about it before I say no!"

"We can't fight them, we can't kill them," Jace huffed as he worked to keep up with her pace, "but we can scare the hell out of them."

"How?"

"You said you thought the greys were elves or trolls, right? Things you believed in? Well what if we can convince these guys that we're angels? That we've come to judge them if they carry out this murder?"

"Angels? That is ridiculous!"

They'd reached the edged of the woods, and Jace wanted to pause to catch his breath, though Tora would have none of it and urged him on. In the dark he could see the time-craft glowing, eerily in the dark.

"This will be perfect!" he said.

• • •

"Absolutely not, it's out of the question!" Aereon looked annoyed, far more than Jace had ever seen him be.

"You have a better idea?" Jace shot back. "Because they're gonna kill this king, and soon! And then we have to start all over, and who's to say that we won't screw things up even more if we wait it out?"

"Your plan will likely 'screw things up' even worse!" Aereon countered.

"Or, it might be just what's needed. Even if we stop them tonight some other way, they'll probably just regroup and try it again in a few weeks, maybe even a few days. What if we could put enough fear into them that they give up on the idea completely, at least until after Edward III is born? Let history get reset. Edward III is born and survives and everything goes back to normal, right?"

"Possibly," Aereon conceded.

"Fine," Jace held out his hands as a plea. "So let me try it. Let Tora and me do this. It might be our best shot."

"It's risky, dangerous, and quite possibly mad," Aereon said, his voice a little calmer now.

"Hey, this whole thing is pretty insane to me!"

Aereon sighed. "We will likely face an inquiry, disciplinary action and a whole lot of trouble, as you might say."

Jace grinned. "Come on Aer, live a little!"

"Do not call me that. Fine, take your seats."

They were soon airborne and drifting upward into the gathering rain clouds.

"Can you track where they are?" Jace asked, feeling ever more impatient, and now not as sure that his plan would work.

"We have sight of them," Tora answered, holding her hand to the side of her head, as if forming a mental picture.

"How many are there?"

"The six conspirators, plus at least twenty others, all on horseback, all armed." She looked over to him. "They are riding toward where Edward's retinue is, and will reach him in less than a quarter of an hour." She turned to look at him. "This is very risky."

"Let's just get in position over them and give it a go," Jace said with confidence, though in secret he wasn't at all sure of his own idea. "I think we can make it work."

"Thinking can get us into a lot of trouble," Aereon said.

"And not thinking will wipe me from existence," Jace answered. "Where are they?"

The greys seemed to move in union with each other, as far as Jace could tell, as if calculating the position of the attackers. Tora closed her eyes for a moment, perhaps communing with them. She nodded and opened her eyes again.

"We are approaching them now," she said. "We will be directly above them in thirty seconds. They have stopped moving. Perhaps this is where they will lie in wait to ambush the king?"

"Then we don't have a lot of time," Jace said, standing up. "We have to do this, and I need you to come with me."

"What?" Tora looked shocked. "Why?"

"Strength in numbers. It will be more impressive if there's more than one of us. They'll think twice before attacking if there are two 'angels.'"

"And you're sure of that?"

"Not at all, but isn't it worth the risk?"

Tora sighed. "If we die, I will never forgive you."

"I can live with that."

• • •

Soon after, Jace and Tora stood at the edge of the craft's door, waiting for it to open.

"You will be descending through low clouds to them," Aereon cautioned, "and you won't be able to see the ground until you break through the cloud line. I recommend a slow descent, to eliminate the chance of disorientation. You can guide the direction of your fall by holding the belt here," he touched Jace's belt, "and concentrating on where you wish to go. You will need to do so to avoid landing on anything, or anyone."

"Yeah, crashing into one of them would kind of defeat the purpose," Jace said.

"I do not like this, not at all," Tora interjected. "I do not hold to these men's beliefs, and find mimicking them strange, at best."

"You don't have to, and strange is fine," Jace said. "We're trying to stop a murder, and that's all that matters, right?"

"We are in position. Are you prepared?" Aereon looked at both of them. Jace nodded. Tora looked down and shook her head.

"Be ready to light this ship up as bright as possible," Jace said.

Aereon stood back. "We will descend as you break through the clouds and increase the craft's luminance by a factor of ten."

At once, the invisible door slid open and Jace looked out into the murk of a cloud at night. It was cold and damp, and wind blew in his face. His heart pounded and he took several deep breaths. He looked over at Tora.

She nodded. "Let us do this and be quick about it."

Jace took one more breath and touched his belt where Aereon had shown him. He and Tora stepped forward and fell into the cloud. It was the strangest sensation Jace had felt in some time, and that was saying something given what he'd experienced in these few days. The air was biting, and he could feel water vapor hitting against his face. He looked over to Tora, who seemed lost in concentration, as she so often was; he envied her.

They drifted downward, a feeling completely unlike falling. Jace looked down into the dark, and could only hope that his plan would work. He felt some shaking, not unlike turbulence on an airplane, and then a blast of wind in his face as he and Tora emerged from the cloud. Above them, the craft fairly burst forth with light, illuminating the whole area. Jace could see some men on horseback, and some dismounted. He and Tora began their descent, trying to stay in unison with each other. He directed his thoughts to control and descend, surprised that it actually worked. Somehow, he could feel Tora's thoughts and presence as well, as if she was guiding them, slowing with each passing moment. The light from the craft illuminated them, making their suits sparkle and shine.

"Good," Jace said to himself.

By now, the would-be assassins had spotted them and were pointing upward, speaking frantically amongst themselves.

"I just hope they don't have arrows," Jace said, though not loud enough for Tora to hear.

The men below now seemed to be panicking. In another few moments, they would be within earshot. And still, Tora guided them smoothly, while the craft above illuminated them in its almost supernatural-like light. It was perfect.

Jace took a deep breath and prepared his performance.

"Merciful Mother of God!" he heard one of the conspirators shout. "What devilry is this?"

"Not from the devil, but sent from on high!" Jace announced in the most authoritative voice. "Hear us and tremble mortals, for we are angels sent from the Lord to warn you."

He glanced over at Tora, just as the craft above let out a brilliant flash of lights, in multiple colors, which must have looked awesome and terrifying to the assembled motley bunch below. Emboldened by their reaction, he descended farther, holding out his arms wide on both sides, a bit like a crucifix, he decided. He hovered a mere twenty feet above the ground and spoke again.

"Cease from this wickedness! How dare you seek to take the life of God's anointed king? You small and hollow worms! The vengeance of God will be upon you all if you proceed with this murderous and sinful act. Damnation and hellfire await you all should you spill even one drop of this king's blood!"

"Listen to him, weak and pathetic mortals!" Tora spoke up in a commanding voice of her own as she floated near him. "The fate that awaits you is far worse than you can imagine. Never-ending torment on the shores of a sea of fire, your pitiful forms impaled on iron stakes, while devils shall dance around you, mocking your agony for all eternity!"

Jace suppressed a smile. *Nice one, Tora!*

Several of the men had fallen to their knees, while some on their horses struggled to calm their animals, who were getting more and more restless. The craft let out a thunderous sound, something like a trumpet blast.

"Hear that, mortals!" Jace continued, pointing above him and enjoying every moment of this. "Hear the sound of the heavenly trumpets! Hear the sound of vengeance! Hear the sound of a host of angels coming to do battle with you, and send you to the punishment you so richly deserve!"

"Flee now!" Tora shouted. "Flee while you might yet find forgiveness. Flee from this place and never think again of this wicked act, and perhaps you shall be forgiven and spared the most horrid of fates!"

"Run away!" Jace ordered. "Run and join monasteries, in order to save your souls!"

Tora gave him a quick side-eye, and Jace worried he might have overstepped. The craft began flashing lights, on and off, like strobes now, something these poor fellows had obviously never seen.

There was a moment, when the conspirators seemed struck with terror and were speechless. Then, three of them rode off in different directions, while the leader's guards began to shout at each other and fled in panic, also bolting off in random directions. Three remained, but two were still on their knees and looked to be praying. Only the leader remained standing, though he looked as if he might crumple over at any moment.

"You," Jace pointed at him, reveling in the payback for getting threatened earlier. "You have conceived this evil plan, and you will be consumed, unless you leave now. Flee from here, and never speak of this moment or this night again, lest we return and send you to eternal damnation!"

The craft let out another series of light flashes from the clouds, almost mimicking lightning. This was enough for the remaining would-be assassins. Without a word to each other, they mounted their horses and sped away, taking no notice of each other, and only wanting to be as far away from here as they could.

Jace let out a relieved breath and looked over at Tora, who gave him another of her almost-smiles. He touched his belt and began to rise up, and she followed along. He looked up to see the craft descending down to them. They drifted up to meet it, with an almost casual air, and soon were standing inside again.

"What is the status of the king?" Tora asked at once, before anything else could be said.

"He and his entourage are about a mile away up the road, heading toward the castle," Aereon replied. "They will arrive there within a quarter of an hour. It is beginning to rain, and it is doubtful they will have seen anything. There is no sign of the conspirators. They have all fled."

Jace couldn't suppress his grin. "So… my plan worked, then? Ol' Jace has saved the day? Not bad for my first time out, eh?"

"It was reckless, dangerous, and could have caused irreparable harm to the timeline and made matters far worse," Aereon said, with more than a little touch of defensiveness in his tone. "You and I both will have much explaining to do back in the thirty-first century. You are lucky to be alive and still solid in the timeline."

"You're welcome." Jace gave him a mock bow.

Aereon turned to leave the small room, but Jace was sure he saw a look of satisfaction on his face.

Jace turned to Tora. "How about you? What do you think? Was it a good idea? I'd say the benefits outweighed the risks, yeah?"

She looked at him with a cool expression and walked past him, preparing to also leave. She paused, but didn't turn around. "I agree with everything Aereon said. It was foolish, reckless, dangerous, and could have had disastrous consequences." She glanced back at him with the slightest of smiles. "Perhaps we can do it again, sometime."

She left without another word. Jace laughed.

. . .

"Look," said Jace to the assembled group of future humans of all kinds: greys, taller beings, hybrids, and those who looked nearly human. Aereon was seated next to Tora nearby. He had the feeling he was standing before a tribunal, but he had no intention of backing down. "We were in an emergency situation. They were going to kill the king right then, and we had to act. If we hadn't, we would've wasted that trip back in time and had to start all over again. Except, I might not even be here, or your scientist for that matter, so I did what I had to do. Yeah it was spur-of-the-moment, but sometimes you have to think on your feet, you know?"

"You knew the risks?" asked one hybrid, a woman he'd not seen before. She looked less human than Aereon, and less friendly, if that was even possible.

"I did, ma'am, but we were out of time, and I think my solution worked pretty well. We scared the crap out of them, excuse my language. We made them think that angels had come to them to inflict divine punishment, and we got them to abandon the plan and never talk about it again."

"And if they do speak of it to anyone," Tora interjected, much to Jace's surprise, "they will be seen as either mad, drunk, or they'll be investigated for heresy."

Jace pointed to her. "Yes, that! See? We stopped something from happening and they won't do it again. At least not for a long time. And all we need is for Edward III to be born, right?"

"What of these nobles, these would-be murderers?" asked another, more human in appearance. "What if some of them do as you commanded, and go and join monasteries? What if there are children they were meant to father, but now will not? Could that affect the time line?"

Jace had no answer, but he was glad when Aereon spoke up. "It is a risk, but a small one compared to what we were facing, I think. I have asked a team of greys to investigate; they can do so far faster with their advanced brains. So far, no issues of significance have been found. If any of the conspirators did take up the monastic vocation, it seems to have had no real effect on history. Perhaps their descendants perished during the Black Death years, anyway."

Thanks, Aereon. Jace forced away a triumphant grin.

And yet, this broke many protocols, one of the taller almond-eyed beings thought to them, in a voice that could have been either male or female. *We have such rules in place for a reason. If we flout them, we risk much, even the undoing of all we seek to achieve.*

The being known as Lyffe responded in thought. *I believe that it is necessary sometimes to take risks. Jace was bold and decisive when he needed to be. We can decry his actions as reckless, or we can see them as a model for how sometimes greater risks lead to greater rewards. The task ahead of us is still enormous, and if we hope to succeed, we will have to be open to changing our ways. Properly trained and guided, I see that Jace could be a valuable ally for future missions.*

"Wait," Jace said, "You want me to do *more* of these?"

"There are multiple anomalies and problems at various points in human history," said the first hybrid. "It might be good for us to correct them, rather than leaving them to grow worse."

"Are these things you've done, or did something else cause them?" Jace asked, a little more harshly than he intended.

"Both." The hybrid spoke to the assembled group. "We must begin to acknowledge our mistakes and seek to correct them. We cannot say that we seek to build a better future if we leave a damaging wake in the past."

"I agree," Ona spoke up. Jace had noticed her when he came in, but was preoccupied with the hearing and had forgotten she was there. "I am perhaps biased in that he is the father of my children, but having met and spoken with him, I now see his presence in them. They will bring his good qualities into their lives and we will be the better for it. If he can be of use to our cause in the future, I strongly support including him in more missions."

There was a general murmur, but most seemed to agree.

"Hang on... do I get a vote in this?" Jace looked around at them. "I kind of have a busy life already."

We would not need to call upon you often, Lyffe projected, *but at certain times your... unorthodox methods might be just what are needed to correct a past wrong.*

"I mean, I guess?" Jace couldn't think of anything else to say. "I'm honored, um, I'll need some time to think about, okay?"

"You have time now," said the first hybrid, "which you didn't before."

"Fair point," Jace said with a shrug.

"If you would like," Tora stood and spoke up, "I can continue with his training. He is fairly useless so far, but I see much promise in him." She flashed him the barest smiles, and he couldn't help smile back.

"If you wish to assume that terrible burden, so be it," Aereon said, standing up, and Jace was certain he saw the hint of a grin on his face as well.

"Glad to know I'm such a hit," Jace joked.

The assembled group began to file out of the room and back into the complex, until only Tora, Aereon, and Ona remained with him.

"You really think this is a good idea?" Jace asked Aereon and Tora. "I'm hardly a superhero, you know."

"You don't need to be," she answered. "Just pay attention to me and you'll soon be as good as you can be, though never at my level."

"Your humility is breathtaking," Jace joked, as she turned and walked away.

"We will return you to your own time, to just after you left," Aereon said. "You and your wife will have some conversations, I suspect."

"Oh yeah," Jace sighed. He put a hand on Aereon's shoulder. "Thanks for everything. For the look ahead, for the opportunity to save the timeline—and myself—and maybe a chance to do some more good."

"I still think you are reckless and irresponsible," he put one hand on Jace's own. "But I'm willing to give you a try." With a sharp nod of his head, he turned to leave.

Ona approached then and held out a thin and fragile hand to Jace, which he took in his own.

"This is still pretty weird for me," he said.

"I understand," she said. "But I meant what I said. You *are* in Cam and Susan, more than just biologically. And I think you have much to teach them, should you wish to see them again."

"I'd like that," Jace nodded. "They're my 'mixed time' children."

"I know they would like to see you again, too." She held his hand for a moment longer. "Farewell for now. I look forward to our next meeting."

Jace felt a sense of acceptance and welcoming from her that was deep and loving. He was grateful for it. "I do, too."

• • •

Jace took a deep breath as he stepped out of the craft and into the dark woods. Aereon had said it was very soon after they left Sara, only the time it took for the craft to leave the area. He walked with determination, still not quite sure what he was going to say. The trees thinned and under the moonlight, he could see Sara standing in the same place she'd been, looking around, as if worried about his absence. Without saying a word, he increased his pace and soon was running toward her. She smiled and opened her arms as they embraced and then kissed. He didn't want to let go.

"Jace," she said after a long moment of silence. "Are you okay?"

"I'm fine," he said, stroking her hair. "It's just been a while since I've seen you."

"None of this makes any sense," she said, looking confused.

"Honestly? It still doesn't to me, either. But I'm working on it."

"We could not have succeeded without his help." He heard Aereon's voice behind him, and turned, surprised to see not only Aereon, but also Tora and the three greys approaching, blurred though they were.

"We have set something right in the timeline," Aereon explained, "something that happened long ago and threatened fundamentally to alter all existence."

"We saved a medieval king from being assassinated," Jace said. "It's… a bit of a long story."

Sara shook her head, looking at them in disbelief. The greys moved nearer, and to Jace's astonishment, they slowed their blur, only for a moment, allowing him and Sara to get a look at them, the classic "aliens" with black, almond-shaped eyes, grey skin, and small stature. Sara let out a gasp, and Jace almost joined her.

He has helped reset the timeline, one of them thought to them. *All may now proceed*, another projected. *He has our thanks*, the third added. And with that, they resumed their blur.

"Yeah," Jace said. "They tend to do that."

"Mom? Dad? What's going on?" Grace and Tom were hurrying up to them, having obviously heard the commotion from when he saw off their beer-drinking intruders. They ran up and he and Sara welcomed them into a group hug.

Jace took a step back and motioned for his new friends to come forward. He smiled.

"Kids, you're not going to believe this…"

ABOUT THE AUTHOR

GEORGE DEPUY IS RETIRED FOLLOWING a 40-year career in higher education. During that time, he worked, most notably, at State University of New York (Binghamton and Utica); University of Wisconsin-Stout (where he served as Vice Chancellor and Provost); UC-Berkeley; and FSU-Panama City. Prior to his time in higher education, he worked at Bell Labs and IBM. He holds a BS degree in electrical engineering from New Jersey Institute of Technology, with MS and PhD degrees from Syracuse University. He is married to Dr. Kathleen Valentine and has three children and seven grandchildren.

Lightning Source UK Ltd.
Milton Keynes UK
UKHW020003221022
410730UK00024B/343